Seizing
the Ivy

Seizing The Ivy
By Barbara Parsons
© 2017 Barbara Parsons

Manufactured in Canada
Designed by Matthew MacKay
Cover design by Aidan Searle, Egg Creative *eggcreative.ca*
Author photograph by Sandra MacDonald

Parson, Barbara
        Seizing The Ivy
ISBN: 978-1-933480-45-9 (softcover)

        I .Title.

PS8631.A777S45 2018   C 813'.6   C 2018-900759-1

        Library of Congress Control Number: 2017961205

Manufactured in the USA

Bunim & Bannigan Ltd.
P.O. Box 636, Charlottetown, PE, C1A 7L3, Canada
www. bunimandbannigan.com

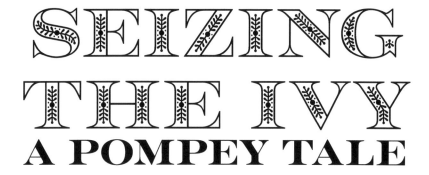

SEIZING THE IVY
A POMPEY TALE

BARBARA PARSONS

B&B

Bunim & Bannigan, Ltd.
Charlottetown, Canada
www.bunimandbannigan.com

DEDICATION

To My Mother
MAUDE
&
My Husband
JIM

TABLE OF CONTENTS

Prelude 1987   1

1   Beatrice   13
2   Plum   17
3   Visiting Ivy   20
4   All Hands To The Pump!   24
5   Ivy In Paradise   29
6   Triss And Delie   30
7   Art   33
8   Dolly   37
9   Juliane   38
10 Glebe Repose   42
11 Ivy Can't Sleep   45
12 Dorita   49
13 Omar   51
14 Lunch In Garcia's Room   55
15 Dorita Again   57
16 Dinner With Plum   59
17 Delie   62
18 The General   63
19 Harbour View Inn   65
20 Annual Glebe Dinner   70
21 Cats   73
22 Crisis   74
23 Glebe Board Meeting   77
24 The General Has A Ploy   80
25 The Battle Joined   82
26 Triss And Delie   84
27 Eviction   85
28 Greenray   87
29 Shadow   90
30 Vigil's End   95
31 Christmas   97
32 Funeral   101
33 Seeking Mother   103
34 A Beige Pouffe   107

About the Author   118

PRELUDE 1987

Visiting old Portsmouth's North End to tend her sister Myrtle; memories of her life there with her late husband, Ralph, and her early days as a nurse, occupy Ivy.

From the bus window Ivy peered at pairs of houses, constructed for veterans of the Great War, in streets named after towns in France like Bapaume and Peronne. On her way to visit Myrtle, her sister, she ruminated over her last visit to Gunner Street. Maw had long gone. The whole area between Lake Road and the Building School had been dismantled! One look was enough.

The approach to North End awoke in Ivy more memories confounded by transformation. Absent, the Hilsea bus garage. Tennis Club a memory along with the all-blue Vita Dry Cleaners. Present the Rathgar Hall minus the ballroom dance academy where Beaty wasted half her life vying for medals. As the minibus idled at the Battenburg Avenue stop, Ivy got caught up in a freezing night long ago and Ralph, old for his thirty years, shivering outside the corner bank.

Making an effort to slot into the present, Ivy got off at the next stop. Vera Rafferty's house gave her another turn as, with Ralph and the Thirties closing in, she excavated Vera's voice: "Close the door for the love of Christ! Don't be one of them open-arsed boggers. So her waters broke? Yer don't know do yer? What the bloddy hell does she think she's doing with her confinement at home?"

Resolutely erasing the midwife, Ivy prayed for grounding in the here and now of the treeless road's endless stone fronts stretching to Copnor. In the grey and misty morning, Myrtle's house stood out, weeds reaching over the wall. Ivy tinkered with the gate and, crouching on the tiled path, fumbled in the aubretia for the doctor's key and opened the door to the hall and Myrtle, in satin nightgown and fur jacket, as if in wait for clarification to a black-tie affair. Ivy staggered through to the dining room to check boiler, kitchen stove and toilet. Paying no heed to Myrtle's cries about a trip out to Southsea to get slippers, she leaned over, gathered up her sister, shunted her to the front room, sat her in the woolly chair, turned up the convector, and put on the kettle.

Myrtle sat up, "Look here, Ive, you heard what I said. I want to go out Southsea way."

"There's bound to be a bargain basement in North End."

"I said Southsea!"

"Could you make it up to the bus stop?"

"Last week I walked all the way up to the end on my own."

"All right," Ivy sighed, "but I warn you, I'm going to have to move you and the camp bed down here. Clothes can go in the hall cupboard."

After fitting Myrtle into the right bra, pulling up her flannel panties, fastening suspender belt, finding a waist petticoat, button-through mauve frock and long brown cardigan, Ivy collapsed in the basket chair. Blinking at the light fixture, she sat up, drained her teacup, knelt down to roll mesh stockings onto Myrtle's bluish legs, went upstairs for a pair of flat pumps, located a white angora watch-cap, then, ready to throw in the towel, sat down again, sighing, "Are you sure we're up to this?"

With Myrtle on the hall chair, Ivy checked back door and electric fire, grabbed her sister and slammed the front door. Arm in arm the pair tottered up the street past lines of cars and the Northern Sec school, where Ivy was to have gone, reaching Copnor Road in time for the bus to quit the stop and pull over. By the time the sisters got seated, they had crossed Copnor Bridge and were gazing out at the Prison, St. Mary's Hospital, the Cemetery and Fratton Park football ground.

When the bus drew up at South Parade Pier, visibility was improving and, with help from the driver, they made it up the steps to the prom and slouched past the pier to enter the first café. Seating Myrtle, Ivy went to the counter, where she collected two milked teas in styrofoam cups and a plastic packet of shortbread biscuits.

Myrtle sat, faded hair sticking up in tufts, gazing beyond the Solent to the eastern tip of the Isle of Wight. Slurping her tea, Ivy decided that Myrtle not only had their father's light eyes and high cheekbones, but some of his ways. With a sigh, she turned her handbag upside down, shook it out and began sorting cards, receipts and whatevers into three piles.

Abruptly Myrtle sat up, "What the bloody hell made you bring me to a dump like this? This is no teashop! Yobbos who never saw a cup and saucer," panting, "never heard the word Teapot! Or Scone! Now we get raspberry jam inside a mini-tub!"

"All right, my love, we'll get a bus to the Circle. No, I better phone for a taxi." Ivy repacked her handbag and zipped it up. "I'll call them now."

"You know what I've got?" Myrtle muttered.

Ivy nodded.

"That I'm terminal?"

Ivy sat down again.

"How long have you known, Ive?"

"Since you were hospitalized."

"Why did they tell you and not me?"

"I can't say for sure, love."

"How could cancer get inside my womb? I never did give birth. Ate what everyone else ate. Had sixty-one appointments at that hospital! All along hearing I'll come through and my hair will all grow back! Then one day ever so casual, they say: 'Not in your case!'"

Ivy shook her head.

"So, here you are with a kid sister at death's door! Only found out last Tuesday! I'm scared stiff, Ive. Where am I going?"

"Some think they're going to Heaven. Look, lovey, wherever you're going, we're coming with you. What you've got to take in, Myrtie, is you're in a crowd!"

"No, I won't," she sobbed, "I'm all on my jack! That bloody consultant had the nerve to discharge me. With a month or two left!"

"Doctor Hanrahan's a decent bloke!"

"Never smiles."

"What's the latest on the visiting nurse?"

"Changed to home help. And she's got sciatica. I tell you, Ive, my life's in ruins. For years it's been going down the drain. Ever since Syd came out the Navy the world changed. Look at North End! Nobody remembers shops like Melanie's and Belmont's. Regent cinema's waiting area!"

"Your track shoes! Dishwasher! What about the new big screen?"

"They took it back."

"We are a bit more comfortable these days."

"We got machines they can't repair. Sloppy help in the house. Look at this street! Loud types moving in, turfing out the toilet, bath and washbasin! A bloody great van labelled Virgin Units rolls up. Piles of plastic sheeting waiting for collection. A few years on they move out. Talking all about celebrities I never heard of. Whiny tunes on their

Sony Walkman. Nobody sings anymore. Nobody whistles."

"Okay, Myrtle."

"Where did the teashops go?"

Ivy shrugged. "Some packed up before the Dockyard closed."

"I come out here last week," she jerked a thumb at the Pier, "went to the end. I'd made up my mind. Slip over the railing! But looking down, the sea looked all brown and ugly. Oh, Ive, I didn't have the guts!"

Ivy looked long and hard out to sea. "I hope we're not out here for another try."

Myrtle tightened her face muscles.

"Try to see it this way, duckie. Every last one of us has got to go."

"But why me? Why now?"

"Think about happy days. Think about Malta."

"Cocktails on board! Me in my hand-sewn evening gowns! Our tennis instructor used to hang out on the esplanade, by one of those funny trees. Just to catch sight of me!"

"Come on, love, let's get out of here and grab some of that cream tea."

●

By the time the taxi dropped them off, the day had turned sunny. Ivy hung out a load of washing, found a pencil and made an outline of Myrtle's feet. Poured out a cup of low sugar cocoa and put on a Victor Sylvester LP. At seven-thirty she made up the camp bed, gave Myrtle her injection, found a pair of shantung pyjamas, and undressed her. At the bedside, scribbling a note to the day nurse and hearing a shudder, she lay down and held her sister till breathing came down to regular. Then, quietly locking the front door, she wrapped the key in foil and hid it in the aubretia.

The trouble with our Myrtle, Ivy decided, as she trudged up to the North End bus stop, is she never had to bother with kids. Probably the fault of that husband of hers. Her looks had started to go under at thirty-nine. I at least had a daughter. Kept me busy for a stretch. Not that she's an asset. Anything but. Never could hold on to a decent job, let alone get married. It can't be that hard. Since Beaty turned forty I heard her mention one bloke only, and he died.

As she crossed the main road, Ralph's image returned with the intensity of a headwind. Gritting her teeth, she caught her breath. *Look*, Ralph was whispering, *it was you who wanted the kid*. Yeh, Ivy thought, and him too proud to let my professional qualifications pay off. Getting us both in the soup.

●

Ralph Gorwick. When did I first see the bloke? Must have been on Ward A6, Surgical. Propped up on four pillows. Kane and Nightingale hovering and Tucker keeping an eye out. Then they hear word old Russell's up the corridor, at which time all three of them melt into thin air.

Bit by bit, it all comes out. Like me, they're going for their finals. With Patient Gorwick paying the fees! Kane, tickled to death in her down-at-heel shoes, knees out of her stockings, gives the word out at supper, ever so casual like, while we're scraping out the last of the custard tart! Nightingale, who can't even afford a twopenny ice cream at Verecchia's, all giggles! Tucker prim as they come.

●

I've always loved hospital life. It's a world I discovered just like that. There was a policeman who used to come in to have his boots stretched in a shop where I worked in Fratton Road. We'd sometimes dive into the next door Lyon's for a breather and sit over a pot of tea. Later I saw him in Kingston churchyard when I'd just started out at St. James's. He told me that all that kind of experience I was getting there, caring for schizophrenics and catatonics and mucking out, could be put to good use nursing sane people. Live in the nurses' home, get board and lodging free, go to classes AND get paid.

At the time, I lived at home at seven bob a week so the idea of board and lodging, all found, knocked me flat. I applied and somehow or other the hospital took me on. I roomed with Kane, petite and man-conscious; Nightingale, large and down to earth; and Tucker, the misery, and we all hit it off more or less. No cooking or cleaning, which made life easier. Mind you, we could be on the wards twelve hours with a break or two collapsing time. I got to know all kinds of patients, some my age, some on their last legs, staff nurse, ward sister, cleaners, doctors, even Matron. The place felt like a convent. It didn't get on my nerves and I wasn't bothered by the smells, well, some I minded.

Get up at six, get to the dubs before the rush, struggle into my blue dress, black stockings, get in the breakfast queue with mug and spoon. On the ward 6.40 sharp. The first year all I did was bedpan pileups, wheel them into the sluice, wheel them out and start all over again. Second year I gave out breakfasts: teas, buttered toast, grapefruit, eggs. But into my third year was when I got attention. Me, first on call for enemas! Last offices! Colonics! They'd ask me how I did them and all I could say was I knew! And after me six months in midder I get a commendation from the Med Super himself on breech delivery! Was invited to accompany Staff on the morning round! Learned how to attend to new cases. Wheel out the dead. I was in heaven!

They called Patient Gorwick 'Moneybags.' The poor bugger had got himself a brand new motor bike. Coming out of New Road a baker's van hits him broadside and a wheel finishes up on his foot. I must say Mr. Barnett did a nice job. Removed two metatarsals. Gorwick was the sort of bloke to tune in to people's anxieties: Kane's love dilemma, Nightingale's mother, and Tucker's sore back. Their worries about finals. And the consequence was, he paid up! I heard plenty about Moneybags, you may depend. Hints about ruby and diamond rings!

Money's not something I cared about. Maybe because it was never mentioned. We always had enough to eat. Our Mum got us decent clothes. Still, if you look around you can't help spotting evidence of big payouts. St. Mary's Hospital didn't get built by slave labour! And neither did the workhouse next door! And what about the prison? A bloody great castle just off the Copnor Road! Barracks with married quarters all over the place: Eastney, Hilsea, the Vernon! What about the Dockyard! Ships out on the Solent! And don't forget dress shops like Belmont's and Melanie's. Yep there's do-re-mi somewhere and not a word said. Funny, that. Well, it didn't worry me one iota because I'd got the sick to attend to. If I'm happy for the first time what else is there?

There they were, Kane, Nightingale and Tucker putting on Patient Gorwick's new suit, delivered by hand, and tailored, if you please, by Lazarus, the city's best. Making a fuss about taking down the screen. Next thing, with a little help, out comes the bloke! I must say it fitted him to a T. No riding up at the back when he lifts his arms! They tried to make him parade outside the screens. But he couldn't put weight on that foot so off the suit had to come. Well, it didn't look like money's one of his hang-ups.

Occasionally on the seven-to-seven shift I'd notice his curly pate, fresh young face and once, when Staff wasn't in sight, I even stopped off for a yarn. He asked me about myself. I said I'd paid me own exam fees, thank you very much. One morning I was walking through the glassed-in corridor where it crosses the grounds on a freezing day, me in my nurse's cloak, red-lined. Because of my sutures I'd just been selected as theatre assistant!! They kept asking me how I did it, how I placed stitches perfectly, correctly. And fast. I just told 'em I got the top Embroidery Prize at school for intricate work. Not only was I feeling all right, I felt big. Big enough to take over as Matron!

That same day up comes Staff and tells me to put a compress on a patient. I get to the sluice, pour out a bowl of hot water, wheel it down the ward reading the charts till I come to Patient Gorwick. I sit him up in bed, put his foot in soak then go to get the acroflavine. When I get back from the dispensary who's there but Staff reading out the Riot Act. I'm the one in the hot water! It goes on the dressing not on the foot!! It had gone all red and swollen. She handed me such a blistering I was shaking all over.

After that he limped round on crutches. A few weeks later, I noticed him in the grounds. With a lot of stammering he told me he'd put in for a late pass and would I be interested in a flick? Well, I knew for a fact the last film at the Tivoli went on at six and by the time I got off duty had supper and changed, it'd be past eight. Still, I gave it some thought. The least I could do. So we went in and had one at The Rose in June. As he put down our drinks, a woman with a low slung-bust came over, introducing herself as Kitty, who, he said later, always used to bring her mother who could sink eight or nine halves of bitter and never get up. From the way Kitty eyed him I could see that there were the times she left her mother home. Afterwards, not knowing what to do, I took him indoors.

With Maw and Pop he worked like a lucky charm. His mother died when he was four, so father and kids moved in with grandma in Adames Road. Brother Tom was on the Roll of Honour and his father and sister died in the pandemic. So he had nobody. To hear our Mum and Dad carry on you'd think he was the heir apparent! How refined, how proper! Fancy someone like him born in Cuthbert Road! Look at his haircut! That suit! You don't see tailoring like that close up! Even our Jack thumped his tail.

They told him he was welcome. A word you don't hear in our street. When he came the next time he brought a bottle of something or other, and I saw our Mum and Dad look at each other and smile. Another first. It's not clear whether he proposed to me or them. All I know is I get a solitaire diamond ring from Samuel's, hat and coat from the Landport Drapery Bazaar, long-sleeved dinner gown from Melanie's, court shoes from Milward's—oh and an umbrella. Our Mum gets a felt hat and a bottle of port. Our dad gets a pipe and a bottle of cognac. And when Ralph takes out the ukulele and plays 'Ramona' you'd think they'd won the Irish Sweep! Nothing like when I sit down to play 'What'll I Do'?

It isn't that I don't care for him, I told our Mum, because I quite like the bloke. Trouble is I'm on the young side for anything serious.

"Twenty-three's not young," our Mum says. "Look around here, look around there, and before you know it you'll be twenty-eight! And then What'll You Do? Eh? You think single fellers grow on trees? Decent ones? All dead and buried! World's full of old maids. You'll wind up one of those who *had* a fiancé, mark my words." She poured a drop of brandy into me tea.

So on my half day off we go to order a gramophone. We must have had a few in Martha Brickwoods because along Charlotte Street there was a sign over the music shop. "Look", I says to our Mum. "Teasy Erms"! I didn't let on I had four five-pound notes in my purse.

I could tell Kane was jealous, although she tried to hide it. Nightingale looked dubious, and Tucker never spoke to me again.

Thinking over my situation, the fact of marriage, not to say the facts of life, which I knew inside out, put me in a panic. We were in the Tramway, corner of Lake Road, private bar, when I told him I couldn't go through with it. Pulled off the diamond ring and slid it across the table.

"You can't mean it," he gasped, putting down his pint.

"Nightingale says marriage isn't what it seems, that domestic life can do you in and it's especially hard on the young. You get hemmed in trying to please other people, making you lose your looks before your time. I am not turning into a drudge! The truth is, Ralphie, I can't face up to giving up one life for another sort of life!"

"It's nerves", he told me. "I feel the same way about commitment. Sometimes I can't sleep. But look, we're friends, we can make a home and maybe a garden. I heard about a little flat up North End way. It's a nicer part, where the best shopping is."

"No," I said. "My roots are here in the Kingston Road. Why don't you take back all those presents and propose to Tucker?"

He wondered how I could talk like that. Said he didn't care what Nightingale has to say about marriage, put his head in his hands, said he didn't want Kane or Staff either! I had to smile. He gulped down most of the best bitter and whispered, Why can't I see he's the one? He'd met all kinds of women in his life, crew members, passengers. Gals from all over. Society ladies. Actresses. "When I'm working on the ocean, first class. It's you only you, Ivy, and why can't you see that?"

I told him I'm no oil painting. But he wasn't having it and insisted that to him, with my brown eyes and black hair, I'm bewitching!! He goes on: "Most of all and I tell you straight, as to character, not one of those nurses can hold a candle to you."

"I'm the one that set your foot back three weeks."

"That's all beside the point. What I'm saying is: You're commanding! You've got power somehow. You can respond to life's challenges whereas others might…just endure."

"I'm not responding to this challenge am I?"

He picked up the engagement ring, "See the setting? Have you noticed it doesn't catch on stockings? And the sealant behind the setting secures the gem in soapy water."

"I still feel like giving it all back."

"Oh Ivy, life can be so exciting and so terrible. After my Mum died, Dad threw in the towel. At fifteen I gave in my notice at Timothy White's, put my age on and joined up. Got recruited in the Gordon Highlanders. Served at Paschendaele and Ypres."

"How you weren't shot I can't think."

"Many's the time I wished I was. I'm here only because Sarge and them looked out for me. They knew I was just a squirt. And duckboard feet and trench fever! Today I look around at people and realize they're not born. Three years in the trenches! You might guess at what that means because you, Ivy, somehow…somehow…you've been there."

"I've seen quite a few corpses if that's what you mean. Laid 'em out. Heard 'em groan."

•

The consequence was we got a special license. Ceremony in Kingston Church. Wedding breakfast for six in a Cunard friend's backyard. I hired a pink silk suit and cloche hat. No bouquet, just a prayer book.

We got a ground floor flat in Battenburg Avenue which I had all to meself when he was away. Ten days at sea, in port for four. I had me hands full. Furnish the place, beg, borrow or steal the thingummies we need to make it homelike. By the time he comes ashore I'd set up the bedroom, more or less, and started on the front room and to me own surprise, me an 'SRN' was still happy. I loved the flat. More space than I'm used to. Busy all day long, sewing cushions, matching tiles and waiting in for deliveries.

When I ventured out the back in the long grass with a fuchsia bush, I hit it off straight away with the gal next door, Rose, who I must have noticed at St. James's! We'd sit on the grass with our tea and laugh our heads off. That infirmary had some good dances in our day.

The rest and change did me good I could tell. Lunch at Smith & Vospers; shopping up Copnor; days at Hayling Island with Kane and Nightingale. Our Mum at the back gate with the dog Alf. Alf showing up on his own!

The third time I met Ralph at Cosham Railway Station, there's him full of beans, with a brand new suitcase and holding me a bit tighter than I like. In the Railway Inn he orders gin and It and horse's neck, opens the suitcase and I get glimpses of three frocks. Two-piece midnight blue, organdy jabot; black crepe flared at the hem; rose-pink poplin, low necked.

On the trolley bus we get home in ten minutes. Tea things on the table: Welsh rarebit, radish and watercress, ginger cake, Lyons tea, Hovis bread and fish paste. Afterwards we went out and had one at the Green Post and in the gardens. I told him the neighbourhood suits me down to the ground especially as the Copnor Road bus goes straight to the hospital.

His dark eyes turned nearly all black at this. "No wife of mine needs to work," he said quietly.

"That's as may be, but I love me work," I told him straight.

"But look at the hours. Leave home at seven, get home at eight at night. That's no life."

Rubbing his eyes, he said he needed a home.

I didn't fuss at the time because Myrtle was getting married to a commissioned gunner and I'd heard of a vacant flat at the curve in the road. And what with the dog's adventures, bus conductors seeing him jump on, straight up the stairs and under the back seat! Getting off at Battenburg or St. Swithun's Road depending on the bus route! And what with Rosie next door, the peace and quiet, and the soft colours. Determined not to take Ralph's ultimatum lying down, though, I spoke up. If he thinks he wants a wife at home then we must have a baby.

He took this with a poker face so I added I have to have something to do. I'd told him straight off I was a virgin and he said he wasn't. But on our wedding night he was just as scared as I was and so we put off any thoughts of intimacy until we felt comfortable. When he went back to sea on the third trip we were still at square one. I don't think it worried him much, and speaking for meself I couldn't have cared less.

I'd take our Mum out to tea at Fuller's, then to the pictures at the Regent or the Shaftesbury. Myrtle moved in at the curve in the road and with Rosie next door we had teas at Smith & Vosper's.

So the year went round. Ralph brought home a gas stove, gramophone, wireless set with five valves and in time I found meself pregnant.

●

At the Green Post, Ivy entered the lounge bar, ordered a half of Guinness and a bag of crisps, went out to the gardens, and sat down trying to push away memories. A deep grief set in. "I'm not doing enough for our Myrtle!" she cried out. "Should have stayed overnight! Her help's only part time"

The sun had moved and still she sat there, snorting and blotting her face. She collected her bag of Myrtle's bits and pieces of sewing, and went for the bus.

1 BEATRICE

Four years later. On a morning in late October, 1991, Ivy's daughter Beatrice, in her friend Delie's flat in London, scratched a spot on her jeans, "At home Mum's mostly been a pain."

"Have you never thought of times when you might have been a pain?" her friend commented.

"She's been ranting since the year dot. You should have heard my father on the subject."

"So, after you get to her door, you turn round and walk out again?"

"Oh no. Had to sit through sagas like the fogey she baths on a Monday afternoon who had the moxie to recommend her to a friend with Parkinson's! It's when she winds down that I get the okay to try out the electric shower. When I come downstairs she asks about the funny noise." Lowering her head, Triss pulled a hand towel from her front pocket.

"And?"

"The funny noise was my aria from *Rosamunde*. What she's saying is…I shouldn't sing."

"You can't get wild-eyed over mother's rating."

"Something snapped. The crocodile brain took over."

On Delie's shoulder, Maya the parrot opened an eye.

•

Beatrice, tall and gaunt, with chunky friend Delie, both in home-crafted T-shirts, sat sipping tea, Triss reliving her plight in filling in E above high C at the Humane Society operetta, and applause making her take stock of her life as plate balancer, cat pan scrubber, designer dog walker, plus glass bottle grader for Smash!

Delie, glancing at the ormolu clock, shook the teapot, "We're talking mother's moods."

"Criticism on octaves, OK?"

With the parrot clawing its way across the T-shirt's message, Any

Allergy Is an Excuse, Delie pulled half a ginger cake from a Fortnum's tin, and broke off a shred.

Triss moved closer, fade-outs on her mind since aunt Mytle's funeral. "Said she's changing her Will."

Delie set down two cups, hacked off slices of ginger cake and, with silver scoop, ladled out chunks of sorbet. The parrot clenched a claw and let out a squawk. Delie whipped her hand and sucked on it, spiked a dollop of sorbet and passed it over. They praised the parrot's aqua-blue crown, light and dark green tail feathers, rose pink speculum till the amber eyes closed.

Triss, hand over teacup, added, "All I did was touch on my rent. But even if I get a lease renewal what are my chances of absorbing an increase? Unless in the fullness of time, I could...look forward to some kind of..."

"Cushion." Delie held a packet of biscuits taut and stabbed it with a cheese knife.

Under the table, picking biscuits up, Triss muttered, "Probably made with beef tallow."

Beyond the sphere of dining table, aspects of affluent past merged with derelict present.

"Vege oil." Delie sipped tea. "What's her house worth?"

Triss breathed hard.

"What sort?"

"Row house." Wiping an elbow on a strip of newspaper.

"Features?"

"Long front garden."

"And the back?"

Triss muttered to herself.

"Backs onto what?"

"Garages."

"Can't be worth more than eighty."

"The end house went for ninety-seven."

"Market's in a slide." Delie scraped the tub. "Look, when parent gets vehement, rule is stand back. Why bother to invent a fiancé?"

"It's less of a rebuff than zero."

"And entertaining yourself in the shower instead of tuning into her."

Triss got up, slouched past the refrigerator, heaved her coat off the door peg and spun round, "I notice your own mother gets shunted in favour of Aunt Romola."

"What I was going to say is, when's the last time you made a fuss of Mum?"

•

At 11.15 AM Triss, next in line at the Waterloo ticket booth, received an otherworldly nudge that the delayed 11.03 fast train at platform 14 was leaving in three minutes. Closing wallet, grabbing day return, cloth bag, umbrella and sunglasses, she scuttled over to the platform–deserted, except for the orange-jacketed porter waving a white plastic bat as the last door slammed, whistle resounded and train butted forward. Triss ran alongside, twisted a door handle, and leapt on.

On the unstained side of the purple seating, with slackened shoulders, she let worries come and go. New cat's pregnancy. Bistro's midnight shift yielding extra for taxi? Sighing, she felt the rocking motion encapsulate, as with a few squeaks and rattles the train sorted out its route.

At stake, Mum's house. Had never thought about Aunt Myrtle's money, actually Uncle Syd's all for Naval relief. Uncle Art and son-in-law Sloane ransacking stacks of mail, old newspapers and port bottles, eventually uncovering a note under the carpet setting out aunt Myrtle's directions. Moving the bed revealed sliding floorboards and a bank book with £150.

•

The train pulled into Havant station with Triss mentally grinding coffee beans to nullify the landlord's charges of cat odour emanating from Mazda, a former champion. At mother's front door, she dithered in the no-man's-land of the front grass, jonquils and narcissi, lulling fears of a repeat of last week's how-d'ye-do.

Visits held to a certain form. Mum, glad-eyed, unbolts door. Triss, hooking bag to hallstand, steps into living room, moves three hand-crocheted guardsmen, and settles on loveseat. Start of sunny period: hard boiled egg in white bread sandwich, Mum fingering wartime badge, holding forth on standards at a certain elder home, tales of Mrs. Pratt's fancy man who will park in Mum's front after she told him straight.

Usually, when Mum pockets badge, adjusts wall print of blackbird, reaches for the remote as sun descends, Triss creeps upstairs, Mother's voice echoing in stairwell: "Where the hell...?"

But this week, ambience softer, they sit down to twelve-grain toast. For some while Triss had not noticed the minor repairs, but now, room scenery changes were apparent. Eventually it came to her that the old dotted carpet had given way to a verdigris fitted which, unobtrusive and devoid of chemical newness, already belonged. This, along with near matching curtains, lent the room a new look, satisfying and unsettling. Low level suites upstairs and outside when the chain pull was making a comeback. Plus talk of porticoes!

"This carpet seems to enlarge the room," daughter observed as they sat down to frozen apple pie and lemon mousse.

"I wondered if you'd notice. After all, in the time left, I might as well grab a bit of quiet enjoyment for meself."

2 PLUM

"How d'ye do?" Jovian Plum half-rose from his desk and extended a breadth of paw. "So sorry to have kept you waiting. Will that chair be all right? Hard enough?"

"A bit bloody hard if you ask me," Ivy replied, pressing the bentwood chair's seat cushion.

He took her umbrella, scanning her outfit: long white cardigan, dress of white poppies on royal blue ground, mid-blue grosgrain hat, chiropodic shoes. Large breasts and arms, ample abdomen and buttocks, hooked nose and intense brown eyes, taking him back to childhood regrets of his mother's bony proportions. The facial resemblance to his mother led him to wonder about exotic origins.

"The Glebe Repose pledge," he began in distinct tones, "is to offer our residents a high standard of accommodation at an affordable rent." He transferred to a breezy style, "So far twelve ladies have applied." He drew in his chin, "I have read your application and it looks promising. You, I believe, are the only applicant born in the area." He clasped and unclasped his hands, "And I see you don't smoke."

"Used to, Mr. Plum. Five Woodbines a day. One with me elevenses, one with me Guinness, one after me dinner and two after tea. But I've put all that behind me."

"And you practised nursing at the Stellarmount Senior Home until quite recently?"

"Part-time like."

"Right up till your eightieth birthday!"

She brought out a big everything-is-all-okay smile.

"And have I got it right that you made a parachute jump?"

"Yis, went on parachute training during the war. Got twelve and six for me trouble. And I was selected out of an elder shortlist to make a memorial jump at eighty-two."

"What? You mean at eighty-two years old you jumped out of an aeroplane?"

"You might have seen me on the *Evening News*. I was part of the original squad to be dropped over Normandy with medical supplies. But those flights got scratched so all the drills were a waste."

Plum clenched his teeth in a half smile, "Didn't you ever feel nervous?"

"Oh, not 'arf! Crossed me fingers and hoped to die. But had to tell meself, I'm in the middle of a line! As a matter of fact, this last jump, ripcord put me into a somersault. Whipped round by the wind and the land coming at me sideways. Next thing, I'm heading out to sea. Then the wind switched and drove me inshore. O' course I had the latest in crash helmets and I'd rolled meself ready for impact. Just missed the breakwaters and finished up at Farlington Marsh in a blackberry bush! Some young feller on a motor bike took his time finding me, gives me a slug of scotch, puts me on the back seat and off we go to base where they lift me up singing, 'She's a jolly good fellow'."

Plum frowned at the desktop. When he raised his eyes, she held him in an unblinking stare. The motherly aura plunged as she leaned forward, flattening one hand on the desk. "I want to move into the place," she told him.

Avoiding bushy eyebrows and nearly black eyes, he made ticks under Attitude, Ambience and Personality, then half-rising in a reflex, end-of-interview gesture, said gently, "The only thing we can do at this stage is let you know."

Ivy stayed put, twisting her neck, then turned aside, staring at the floor. Sitting down again, Plum considered the shine on her hawklike nose, powdered and rouged cheekbone, youthful essence, way of skirting preliminaries. Eyes on him, she struggled to her feet, chin against chest, made an about turn, tramped over to the fireplace and stood steady on the fender, elbows on the mantelpiece.

Plum mused on her figure, which he decided was a large size in miniature, fiddled with her application, examining her tight, austere handwriting. "I see," he said, "we're missing one entry under Recreation. I wonder if I might enquire about it: RECREATION."

Ivy closed one eye and revolved her jaw in a chewing motion.

"Like games, Mrs. Gorwick. Golf, tennis, that sort of thing?"

She stepped off the fender and began pacing, shoulders bent, hands behind back, raising one side of her head, "Never played sports in me life. Wait! I tell a lie! Once I went ten-pin bowling at the senior men's club. I matched the top score and the bloke never asked me back!"

"Ah. Well what about things like boating, swimming?"

"Oh no. Hate the water. And lived all me life at the seaside! Why, is there a swimming pool in the 'Ome?"

"Heavens no," Plum cleared his throat. "Although we wouldn't rule out the odd visit to a leisure centre." His smile faded into concern as he joined her by the window, "Tell me, in your widowhood, has solitude ever been, um, trying?"

Ivy scratched her neck, "I can manage on me own if that's what you're leading up to. Staying in nights sixteen winters and me own 'ome don't feel too friendly these days. Once my hub was gone, life had another one of its changeovers. When I started work at fourteen, the world was full of boys. Once I was widowed, all I could see were more and more women. Now it's all plants." Standing astride, she flexed her knees, "Recreation! What with house, hub, hospital and daughter, in those days I dint have two minutes to meself nor, might I add, two pennies to me name. On night duty I cut out dresses from memory. One Christmas I sang from the *Chocolate Soldier*," she stood to attention. "Brought the 'ouse down."

3 VISITING IVY

On New Year's Day, Triss's visit to mother promised to be without incident: irises about to burst. Baked potatoes and sprouts on the serving hatch connecting dining area and kitchen.

"Since Dad died things have been far from easy," Triss shouted as she raised the dropleaf table.

"No," mother agreed. "But in the warmer weather I'll get out. Off-peak trips. Bin places I never could get to with him. Like me trip to Arras to visit the tunnels and find your uncle Tom's grave."

"I ought to do more."

"Don't lose any sleep. You got your life to lead." With Ivy's description of plantings at an Ypres graveyard, a measure of content settled over the tea-table.

After a five minute silence, Triss looked up to see mother not eating. "Where did you manage to find this?" Ivy asked. She held up a jar of tofu spread.

"The Co-op had a special."

"I burnt the frying pan twice!" mother burst out.

Triss reaching under the hatch, patted the kitchen surface for the teapot.

"Can't seem to cook for meself without dropping stuff all over the shop." Ivy looked up in vexation. "Coming downstairs the other morning, half the banisters disappeared!"

Triss, crunching on celery and tofu spread, poured tea.

"I mean it this time." Ivy's eyes loomed large behind the bifocals.

Triss let an interval pass to empty her mouth. "Mean what?"

"I'm going to have to move."

Triss gazed beyond the lean-to cyclamen plants beyond the back fence. "Move did you say? Where to?"

"A residence, of course."

Triss placed a digestive biscuit at the edge of her plate, muttering,

"Only a month or two ago didn't I understand the last thing you'd give up is Acorn Terrace?"

"I'll have to won't I?"

"The paper says the housing market dropped out the bottom."

"Eh?"

"Remember Mrs. Welles' house? If you want to stay in her range, you'd do better to hang on until things recover."

"I can't worry meself about that." Ivy tapped the table with her fork, "How can I cook me dinner if I can't see!"

They sat in a non-eating silence on either side of the serving hatch hung with picture postcards and crested teaspoons.

"You've never mentioned a move," Triss said softly.

"It's being forced on me, annit?"

"There's no shortage of agencies to arrange meal delivery."

"There's a place opening up. I applied and I've been waiting to hear."

Triss peeled fibres from a celery stick.

"They don't call it a 'Ome'." Ivy chewed on veal and ham sausage. "I got a bit of paper here somewhere. Two mills and I get me own breakfast. It's along the London Road. After all, I sez to meself, if they can't accept me, I'll just have to put up with staying home with mills on whills won't I? In fact," she added, squirting mustard on the sausage, "I took a ball of chalk over there. Had a nice chinwag with Mr. Plum and now he's phoned to say I'm accepted."

Triss transferred the digestive biscuit back to the centre plate. "But just this minute didn't you say you're waiting to hear."

"No I dint say anything of the sort. What I said was I have been waiting to hear. Not, I am waiting to hear, because they *have* accepted me. Try to concentrate." Ivy shook a bottle and poured out salad cream, "Mr. Plum's picked me and nine other ladies. Coming from all over the place. There's a Clem, an Eve, and a Prue if I remember rightly. And I trained with a committee member's mother, Hilda Gittings. I forget the daughter's name. Dorita. Something like that. And another three coming."

Triss stared across the dining space through the french window beyond the back fence to the tangled TV antennae and line of garages, muttering, "You're getting out is what it amounts to."

"Yis." Mother ate with concentration, chin close to plate.

"Have you gone and put the house up for sale?"

"No, but I shall have to."

"It may take a year to sell. And in today's market it'll fetch a knock-down price. Are you geared to accept a figure like seventy?"

"Mr. Craswell came round to give an estimate and he said I should ask... what did he say? Sixty-nine or was it fifty-nine? Anyway, there's nothing for you to worry about because the Social Services pay me rent at the residence until the house is sold, then I pay them. The work-men'll be out of the 'Ome in about eight weeks. I had a look inside. Just through the window, like. They couldn't show me round the place because of the falling masonry."

Triss watched mother point the tea spout in her direction, then closed her eyes. "I wonder if you've given any thought about what leaving your home might mean? You and Dad moved in when I was little. Imagine life in a bedroom. No hall, no living room, no garden."

"There's everything in that house. I got a plan of the rooms some-where."

"No space to call your own."

"It's a bloody great barn of a place! Have you ever seen a sixteen bed-room house without lounge or garden?"

"What about all your things?"

"I shan't miss 'em for the simple reason I'll be taking 'em with me. You mustn't be such a worry guts." Ivy leant forward, pronging the ta-blecloth with her fork. "All my life I've looked after others, given ser-vice, and now's me chance to be on the receiving end." She tightened her eyes, "That Mr. Plum is ever so nice. He says what's to stop residents taking taxis into Waterlooville to get their hair done. Rides down to Pompey Guildhall. Bridge drives. Day trips to London. One woman plays in golf tournaments. I'll never have mills alone again, never be by meself at night, always have someone to go out with." She stabbed the last end of sausage, pushed it around in the salad cream and packed it into her mouth, mumbling, "I'll be among friends."

●

"Bear in mind," said Delie, as she, Triss and six dogs lurched through the square's revolving grille, "even if your mama says she must get out, deep down she may have doubts. Ask yourself, Has she or hasn't she thought it through?" Delie bent over doggie clean-up and the parrot opened one eye. "I'll never forget Mama going limp at the prospect of emptying the larder. But when the time came round we got the word to collect paintings and stuff like the Bokhhara carpet and Maya thrown in. The whole thing was relatively painless because she was beyond. It seems to me your mama hasn't yet reached that stage. I mean if the banister disappears one morning does it follow that it will every morning? Has she mentioned it since?"

Triss shook her head.

"QED."

4 ALL HANDS TO THE PUMP!

Bare hedges and trees, Wednesdays came and went. Ivy and daughter toured the Guildhall Square, Old Portsmouth pubs, Clarence Pier, winding up on the Ferris wheel.

But one afternoon, Ivy sat on her stairs and pressed for the umpteenth time the redial button on her new telephone. After prodding, the operator at Belgravia Relief reported no Beatrice in the building. Several minutes wait produced an operator at the Humane Society who referred Ivy to another number with a recording: "For Appliance Collection, press One. For Glass and Metal, press Two." Pressing Three, to hard rock, she listened to directions on preparing kitchen waste. She pushed buttons until on came Triss's far-off voice: "I'm on my way out."

"That you, Beaty? Get yourself over here at once. Pack a bag."

"How did you find this number?"

"No matter how. I want you here."

"I'm due at night work at six."

"Pay attention. An interested party has shown up. A dago...The house! Keeps finding fault. Hole in me front gutter. He can repair it can't he? He's a man! I've accepted seventy-two including carpet and curtains. Art's coming with me to the solicitors. Qualified? Supervises a meat-packing plant. Hello...hello? Beaty, where are you? Come back! Salvation Army's been. Took the surplus! All I got to me name is stuff for one room. If I don't go flat out it'll go to the next name on the list. And what with me eyes and all it'll have to be the Stellarmount at twice as much."

After three hours sleep and one on the train, Triss toiled up her mother's staircase. The Waste Depot manager was allowing one day off at half pay and a colleague had lent her his wife's rail pass. Her friend Delie was to enquire if their contact, Fitz, might agree to service the cats. On a radiant morning, mother's front garden showing signs of life, droplets of dew flashing the spectrum, convalescent cherry tree. Ivy, in a mustard sundress, hoisted into the driver's cab, proclaiming to the street, "Thank Christ I'm out of it!"

Later that day, corsets slid off the new divan's plastic cover as Ivy, hair tightly curled, shouted directions, "No, not that window! Does the door look like a wardrobe?!"

Triss wrinkled her nose. "That carpet smells chemical. I wonder they didn't select a quieter colour scheme."

"I chose for that carpet meself and paid for it."

"Not like the verdigris one at home."

"That was the agent's idea."

Throbbing started up in Triss's head.

Ivy tugged on a pair of louvred doors to a double sink, shelves and mini-stove. "I'm going to be comfortable, Beaty. Look at your dial! Can't you try to look on the *braight saide*? They say that about Christmas babies. Get yourself downstairs and find the carpet sweeper and my box of pills."

The housekeeper, aged about twenty with slim figure and chubby face, stood flattened against the front door's stained glass. "I'm Garcia Jones," she lisped. "You must be Ms. Cash's daughter? No? Let me have another go! Mrs. Gorwick's?" Young removal men, grinning, scraped past as she plastered stickers with room numbers whispering to Triss, "We're taking a breather. See you on the patio."

No sign of Mum's pill box, but carpet sweeper riding upstairs, Triss squeezed past mounds of bedding, following the aroma of coffee. In a kitchen that had never seen food, an elder with slender figure and aged face inspected the dishwasher while another, unplugging the coffee-urn, nearly overturned it. Trailed by the two fretful elders and Triss, Garcia trundled through the large print library where a third elder with stubbly haircut and WRAC regimental pin sprang up to throw open the french doors.

"Sit here, Ms. Gorwick," said the young housekeeper with fifty-year-old presence as she lined the trolley up to a deal table.

Triss, sinking into a lounger, thanked the All for glass veranda, overhead clematis, breezes ruffling the pampas grass, rolling lawn, sliver of a brick path.

"Black, white or iced?" Garcia was calling from under the umbrella. "I told Mr. Plum about putting food waste out with newspaper and leaving it to turn into black gold!" She looked round at the timid faces.

"How is that, my dear?" asked Prue, the small lady.

"Just put your finger there if you would be so good, Beatrice is it?" said Clem, the short-haired sergeant. "Well, Prue, it's all thanks to organisms. No see'ems."

Wavering over coffee, Triss was surprised to hear "soy milk." Entranced, she tuned in to Prue's account of the vixen gorging on a pile of her blue cheese scones.

With Prue, Clem and Evie making bets on fox camouflage, slow thumping on the library door went unnoticed through talk of black legs and red hindquarters melting into the pyrocanthus, until the french door gave with a clatter to reveal the hunchback.

Garcia raised a coffee mug, "Just in time, Mrs. Gorwick."

The newcomer produced a new kind of smile, wide and iffy. "Nothing's where I think it is. The worst of it all is me reading glasses. Nowhere in sight."

"They will emerge," rejoined Clem the sergeant, "rarely before their bidding!"

Ivy prodded Triss, "So where's my pill box?"

"We're discussing the fox's diet, Ivy," said Garcia with a mother's smile. "Dog or cat biscuits? Which is the more digestible?"

Triss squeezed Ivy's arm, "Don't fret Ma, the Bissell's on your landing. Along with your pills."

Prue, the tiny lady, patted Ivy's other arm, saying in an artless way, "I'm not admitting chaos into my universe. If the room looks a wreck, Let It Be. So let's sit down and try some fair trade coffee. Ivy is it?"

Ivy, jerking head at daughter, did a three-point turn, clumped through the library and, mouth working, rode up the staircase. Triss followed, puzzling over the new smile. "These are really nice people," she sighed, holding the fire door.

"Sitting around jawing like you got all the time in the world. You always were an unreliable bitch."

Triss, putting the Bissell down, announced, "I doubt you'll do much carpet sweeping here."

"You don't half talk rubbish."

"There's bound to be someone who comes to clean."

"These pills are not mine. I said BOX not bag."

Returning with the First Aid box, Triss noticed Mum padding about the room with a magnifying glass, sighing, "When oh when are you going to ditch your punk phase?"

"My what?"

"You heard."

"I am not cousin Juliane."

"Young Juliane's not punk. None of Art's side are. It's you with your frizzy hair. Multi-coloured tights, skirts up to your crotch. You worried your father to death."

Triss unpacked blindly. Mother threw down the magnifier, tottered over to the window and, against the light, shoulders hunched, slowly swivelled round, eyeing the carpet. "Somewhere along the line you changed," she declared, flexing knees, chest stiffening, and, like the Queen of Spades, leaning forward at a remarkable angle, seemingly kept from toppling by invisible strings. "I ask myself," she added, "what you're cut out for? I dint encourage you to go into nursing because patients under your care might conk out before their time. You got no interest in kids so you'd be a hopeless caregiver. I thought the one thing you might do is clerical work but when you clock in dressed like skid row, no wonder you never get a second look!"

Hands behind back, she turned her body round, "You act retarded and I have to face the fact that I gave birth to a nobody. Other gals do things with their lives. Look at Helen Pratt, manager of a supermarket chain. You can't even hold a steady job! Out of the types you've consorted with you'd think there'd be one who wouldn't drop dead at the idea of marriage. Like that Eyetie! That was a bloody strange business." She resumed pacing. "It's not that I think you're queer. All I know is you haven't turned out right. Out of the three or four schools I sent you to, one must have been for the dim and weak-kneed." Ivy flexed her own knees, "Nice mouthed and toffee nosed." She came closer, "In a coat covered in cat hair, you're not going to get a second look. Now works on a tip! You kept that quiet, dint you?"

Over her mother's head Triss stared through the net curtains at a trio of slender conifers wavering among the sounds and smells of traffic.

"Your trouble is you never took notes from me."

•

"No," mumbled Triss at the bus stop, "never took notes from her. Never hankered after a dozen pairs of stays and a potbelly. If I make it to eighty, will my hair sprout cotton wool? Will a dentist sweet-talk me into multiple extractions on the cheap? I can answer why her Nobody feels incapable. It wasn't the School for Dimwits, more like the Ivy Gorwick Reformatory." In her monodrama Triss missed the fading light's amber tinge so that, hyper-ventilating at the bus stop, a lightning flash jolted her into the now, along with thunderclap and warm raindrops down her back. Pulling out a rainhat, she muttered, "That Mum did not take after *her* mother is my hard luck."

A hologram of Grandma Floss, known as Maw, took shape in the slanting rain. With braided white hair, ankle-length print overall, gold Mother pin, Floss looked the archetypal grandma, planted beside Grandpa Omar and a dish of prunes. Holding a cottage loaf face-up, she'd be sawing off a doorstep, folding it in melted butter. Triss had suspected the grandma act, since even a study of her munching revealed glimpses of past loveliness, merry eyes, curved mouth, touch of the Irish. And the celebrated nose! Pursued by tailors, sailors, proctors, doctors, brokers, stokers, con men, journeymen, Bob Hope's father, over fences, through rock gardens, down alleys, past the laundry to the misty glass of the bar door, and Herself presiding over the Bottle & Jug. Wrinkling the exquisite nose, widening the amber eyes, Floss bent and punched Omar's newspaper, with an injunction not to finish up her plate of *pruins*.

There was the day Triss found drops of blood on the floor and Maw, cutting out a poultice to serve as napkin, singing to herself lyrics Triss couldn't piece together, like keeping a halfpenny inside the lingerie. She'd given up guessing why Beauty had wasted itself on a crusty marine sergeant until the day, dropping in, she found at the red plush table a sallow woman calling herself Millie, with a frizzy-haired daughter, Nelly, crowing, "I'm I' married! For me engagement present I chose to coom down 'ere to see me Gran." Turning to Maw, "Oh Gran, I bin hearin' about yo all m' life. If y'only knew 'ow loovly it is to see yo at last!" Millie was unmistakably a swarthy, puffier version of Maw in her fifties. Her looks rescued from insignificance by the lines of her nose. Recalling all this in the driving rain, Triss acknowledged with relief that Ivy's looks never could have conjured up any kind of skeleton.

Out of the mist a bus glided up, ejecting a passenger. Fishing over-long for her return ticket under the driver's sullen eye, Triss made for the one vacant seat and, among the dreaming passengers, began to sense a kind of reassurance, a place in the human family.

5 IVY IN PARADISE

The dining table at Glebe Repose had been moved parallel to the french windows windows. Residents, spotting place cards, sat down to the inaugural lunch, chatting and laughing. There was a brief silence at Ivy's appearance, which might have served as prelude to grace.

Garcia wheeled in the trolley and set soup tureen and bowls down on the table for Clem to dispense.

"I understand," Hope began, "that you are from Wiltshire."

"Oh yes," Clem replied. "Grandfather bought a thousand acres there in 1890 and built a dwellinghouse called Cloisters."

"I may have heard of the name. Wasn't the site near to 600 BC barrows?"

"We had to sell off part of that."

"My father taught at a public school," added Hope. "Not far from Devizes. The name was…what was it? Ah yes, Downsmere."

"What a coincidence!" cried Lila. "One of our cousins went there. Our own school wasn't far off. Drillinghurst. Papa preached at the adjoining church."

"Well, ladies," said Prue, "I'm short on relatives, just one grandniece who works in some commodity or other. What about you Ivy, what's your story?"

"Worked in hospitals most of me life. Started out at fourteen as a skivvy in a fish shop."

Prue leaned over to put an arm on Ivy's shoulder, whispering, "Join us on the patio for a game of Scrabble?"

Ivy turned round with a shrug, "Might as well." As she struggled up and pushed her chair aside, she mouthed words to Prue, who put a hand to her ear. Ivy then repeated in a slow, emphatic tone, "Sounds like the inmates make a lot out of little."

With fixed grins the residents paused in their reminiscences.

6 TRISS AND DELIE

In seven years, only one member of the multi-cat household had resorted to statements in the bathtub. As a precaution Triss left water standing. In her bathrobe, scooping up a foreign body she left it on the bathtub shelf where, fiddling with tentacles, it sought out its cranny. The bathroom, hardly bigger than a shower stall, had a ceiling high enough for her to hrivele to running water.

After an attempt at "The Soldier Tir'd," muscles afloat, she lay wondering what points Mum might had taken from Grandpa Omar aka Pop, who, sitting barrel-like, tipped his chair back to lift a steaming kettle from the coke fire, his bluish eyes raking the table and pipe on breadboard, pouring tea dregs for Jack, the small grimy canine. Transfer to the kitchen sink, jaw taut against the wobbly mirror, scraping stubble with the cutthroat.

A dingdong at far remove broke up the reverie. In a rush of warm water, Triss sprang up and pushed the casement, shouting, "Now what?"

Delie, backing up to the kerb, cried, "I came early on purpose."

"Do you mind hanging about?"

"Fitz is here."

•

Fitz, known at his Camden bar as the Bouncer, sat phoning in a corner of Triss's living room, while she and Delie held fast to ginger pop bottles as cats lean and battletorn tomcats, boat-shaped mother cats, and grown kittens, picked their way over shoulders and down chests, congregated on knees, butted heads and settled on sofa arms.

Unravelling the nearest sphinx–Mother Courage, misshapen and bony–Triss announced, "Emcee's coming through at last. With shots and abscess draining at a discount, but I'm still short five dog walks on the rent… No. Wire brush the throat from chin, down belly, avoiding udders and the tail area."

"The house was sold then?" Delie murmured.

"Brush against the growth."

"What did she net in the end?"

"Dropped the price to absorb repairs so she's left with seventy one." Triss set Emcee down and lifted an emaciated white male with battered ear, gray tail, and loud purr.

"Have you met the Colonel? Paddington Station, platform 3. Stool has recovered. Finally."

"You couldn't block the sale to a meatpacker?"

"Freezer department supervisor is the code."

"You don't seem at all…hysterical."

Winding both arms round the Colonel, Triss scratched her chin on his large head, "Faced with *force majeure.*

Delie, frowning, teased Piper's tender neck, "How long will it take Mama to adjust?"

"Adjust? To meals at a polished table? Oval bathtubs?" Triss released the Colonel and took up a weighty brown tabby, "Try out the watercolours, Crampon? Sing *Im Paradisum*? My hangup may be What if? Like an emergency!"

"There always uncle."

Triss carefully unhooked Crampon. "Did bits of shopping the once. Bought mince instead of mints. Kept the change." She stood the tabby on his hind legs, brushed his belly up and down to loud purring, carefully returned him to the rug and took up a brownish-black, slit-eyed shorthair. "How now Lover Boy?"

"Is uncle the Miser?"

Valentino settled in a close embrace. "The title fits. Out of the blue Art moved back from East Anglia to his roots. Mum hadn't seen Art since Dad's funeral. I had fantasies of them watching the Cowes Regatta together. But visits were blue moon. One of Mum's gibes about Art's daughter Marlina hit home." She cut around a furball with scissors. "Rudy sweetheart, please!"

"I see twenty," said Delie.

Triss pulled a notebook from behind a cushion: "3 black, 4 tuxedo, 2 brown tabby, 1 calico, 2 ginger, 3 gray, l all white, 2 white with patches, 2 recovering. Wait a second. I see five tuxedos! There's Fred: white front, three boots, one shoe; Junction: white bib, bikini, four shoes; Ritzie: white front and two boots; Tailsie: bikini, one boot, two and a half shoes. And here's number five! Look here, Fitz! What do you think you're up to?"

Fitz, a slender, black New Yorker in a three-piece suit, replied, "Look at the symmetry. Bib, halter and bikini! Two identical front shoes, ditto identical hind boots. A champion. And loving. Okay, ladies, lemme clarify! Grant me a chance to put him in the picture! I had a 20 kilo bag of kibble plus a 25 kilo bag of clumping litter delivered to your basement locker. Why? 'Cos this ain't no ordnerry cat. Here's the scene. A dear friend, Marty, hospitalized Thursday, dies on Friday. I can't take Sylvester home anymore. Why? I got two kitties in street recovery plus I'm minding a wolfhound cross, and Moxie's back is up."

"You could leave him where he was."

"Darling, the apartment is on the market plus Marty was behind in his rent. No lemme finish. I don't ask favours. Left my dues on your dresser."

Later Triss, searching for notes among papers on her chest of drawers, came across a folded money order. Opening it out, she held it to her breast gasping, "I always knew that place was a whorehouse!"

7 ART

Having adjusted the table lamp to the right slant, sought out reading glasses, removed shoes and stockings, toe separators eased out and toe joints massaged, Ivy had just lifted the magnifying glass when her brother's marbled face appeared round the door. It was the Saturday of the spring equinox.

"Oh hello," she said in a minor key.

"Hello, my lover." Art, in twill shorts and checked sport shirt, glanced at half-empty packing boxes. "All right are we?"

"Bearing up."

"Got a seat for Artie then?" He rubbed his hands in a breezy, friendly way.

"Sit on the commode if you like. Or there's me garden seat behind the door."

He snapped the alloy and canvas chair into position. "Wotcha been up to?"

Ivy cocked her head at the pile of boxes. "What do you think?"

"How are the other ladies?"

Ivy raised her eyebrows. "Awfully *dignifaid*. The sarnt major is one of the Wiltshire Boondoggles." She reverted to her own burr, "One got a cat, one seems simple, twins on their last legs. One got a rich son called Brarn."

"What about the food?"

"I don't know how me gut'll stand up to the spices. That housekeeper must be a few pence short of a pound."

"Got your papers in order?"

Ivy twiddled her hearing aid. "Papers?"

"Your PAPERS."

"Pile them up for the cleaning woman to take."

"Papers. PAPERS about the sale of the house. SALE OF THE HOUSE. Look, Ive, I brought you this." She stared at his sandy head and sun-reddened neck as he rooted around in a plastic carrier, pulling out an accordion file. "Present for yer."

"What would I want with that?"

"To put your papers in."

"What papers?"

"I told you. Your bankbooks and things. Your WILL."

"Oh."

"Now what I've done is this. I made a few files, one for your bills, one for bank statements, so get your papers out." Grumbling, Ivy bent down to reach into a bedside drawer and dragged out an envelope.

"That's good. Now when I call out 'Banking' you hand me the letter and we'll put it in Banking."

"I can't be bothered with all that now, Art." She put the bulky manila envelope back on the coffee table.

He lifted the flap, "Is the Will in here?"

Steadying herself against the wall, she padded over to her kitchen unit and brought out another envelope, long and stone coloured.

Art extracted the Will and scanned it, running a finger down the margin, then looked up. "After all expenses and costs are met, house goes to Beaty. Well, I think now's the time to do a redraft, don't you? You know you've got to change it. You don't have the house any more. You can't leave it to Beaty or anyone else because YOU WON'T HAVE IT TO LEAVE."

"No, I won't."

"So we'd better draft a new Will and take it round to Mr. Crate. DRAFT A NEW WILL."

Ivy stroked her chin. "Well, I would be grateful for your help. But all I got to do really is cross out the word 'house' and write in 'residue' which is what Beaty'll get if there is any, which I don't expect there will be."

Art frowned, then grinned, "Only a few months ago you were talking of cutting her out."

"I doubt there'll be anything to cut out."

"Don't I get a mention then?"

"You?" Ivy scoffed. "One foot in the grave, the other one on a bar of soap."

"Come on, Ive. What about a few bob for the little brother?"

"Look at the weight you put on since you had that op. Do you pee any better now?"

One side of Art's face twitched.

"Didn't I hear Doll say you had to go back in?"

"It was the ordeal to end all ordeals being trussed up on Felix Ward. I didn't think I'd make it."

Ivy nodded with understanding.

"Then on my last day the lady doctor making the round says to me 'All this needn't affect 'our sex life.' I told her, 'Don't 'ou worreh about me sex life. That won't come up for review until the year two thousand and twenty-five!' "

Ivy spat out one of her rare laughs. "It looks like I'll be the one to survive you. I may be a few years older but being a woman counts these days."

Art uncrossed his legs. "Getting back to the Will, perhaps you'd like to leave Juliane a few shekels. She's been ever such a good kid."

"Which one's that? Not the young one."

"That's Marlina. It's Juliane, the one that looks like me. She needs help."

Ivy picked at her cuticles. "Why should I care?"

"Why not?"

"She's your kid, not my kid. Beaty'll need every penny. Never seems to have enough for basics. Has to go around cadging hot water."

"Beat got savings. Stands to reason. If she buys any clothes at all they come from the Nearly New. She's a lot like Myrtle that way."

"Myrtle!" Ivy stroked her prominent nose. "I dunno so much."

"I mean," Art wrinkled his cheek and scratched it, "if she can't spend time caring for you, in her absence I'd have to be your next-of-kin."

"Well, I suppose there's something in that."

"Got no family of her own. That so-called fiancé was probably married. And if worse came to worse you'd want me to have Power of Attorney."

"That's as may be," Ivy scowled. "But that wouldn't mean I'd have to do anything for Juliane just because she's the spitting image of you. What has she ever done for me?"

"She might be doing something for you while Beat's up in Manchester marching for cats' rights. Juli had to give up her job for the twins. She could have been on her way to management."

"No one asked her to mess with fertility diagnostics. She's lucky she dint wind up with quads."

"Now Sloane's worried about downsizing at the egg processing plant.

I tell you, Juliane must have cash," Art spoke into her ear, "for her sanity."

"I'll give her five," said Ivy with finality. "I'll admit she's some improvement on that young Marlina."

"Five thousand! That would be a help."

"I mean five hundred."

"Five hundred won't last a fortnight. Come on, don't be a shonk. Make it four."

"Four thousand quid! I'm buggered if I will."

"Make it three then."

Ivy looked up from putting on sandals prior to going down to Scrabble, "I won't spend more than two. Why should I even spend that?"

"It's a kind of insurance, annit?"

8 DOLLY

Dolly, mopping the kitchen counter, muttered "Twenty to four" when Art, bathed in sweat, tipped groceries on the floor.

"Popped in to have a yarn with our Ive," he explained, "about the Will."

Dolly, large and dark-eyed, squeezed the J-cloth, "Why must you keep nosing into her affairs?"

He rubbed his hands, "Where's me dinner then?" At the dining table inserting his knife under peas glued to the plate, he mumbled, "Wotcher mean nosing? She needs my help."

"You won't be in her Will."

He gnawed on the pork bone. "No mortgage on that house. Remember we're four and she's only one."

"She's two," Dolly reminded.

"I oughter find out her exact rent."

Dolly got up to beat crumbs and dust off the sofa.

"Remember the day she showed up in the rain carrying on about Beat? Leaving her out of the Will! I'd never seen our Ive that definite! Ever see Beaty put herself out for her mum? Take her on a trip?" He scraped the knife round the rim of his plate. "You don't want to agonize. The Will's got to be changed and Juliane will get a bit. That much she promised."

"In that case both girls ought to get something."

9 JULIANE

Mumbling about a dearth of airing cupboards, Ivy stamped into the utility room, piled in the washing, inserted coins and started the machine as Aggie, wrestling with a load, dropped half on the floor, calling out for change to Ivy, who slapped a handful of coins on the counter. Aggie's machine stayed mute. Sighing, Ivy threw down her nursing magazine and reinserted the coins. As the washer clicked into action it shuddered dangerously, Overload button flashing. Rushing to turn it off, Ivy elbowed Aggie, who lost her balance. With Lila in the doorway, Aggie started whining, "Don't let that woman anywhere near me."

"What on earth…?"

"She knocked me over."

Ivy leaned over to knead Aggie's shoulders, then pulled on her legs. "Now," she ordered, "let's get you straightened out," pressing Aggie's shoulders. "Any pain here? No? Well then, let's get you up!"

"My sister is in shock," Lila said with a flinty stare.

●

Ivy returned to her room and was just settling on the couch as Juliane, thinner edition of her father, appeared. Settling on Ivy's commode she brought out gillyflowers in crepe paper along with regrets for absence at auntie's birthday.

"Birthday! It's the middle of April. You're only a month late."

"Oh well, happy happy. I only dropped in to leave off some tea." The niece sat to attention as auntie made a tally of teas served daily at table and in her room. Jerking a thumb at the gloxinia in bloom, Ivy added, "From your little sister."

Disregarding the fanfare of vermilion trumpets, the niece, one foot on the coffee table, twirled a lock of hair, sniffing, "On my way to pick up the twins from playgroup and I just thought you'd like one or two pics."

Ivy opened the photo packet, shuffled through and slid them back across the coffee table.

"Kids cost a bomb," Juliane sighed.

Ivy looked unconvinced. "Pass me those batteries. No, as you were. Nope, if I turn up the sound it's still not right. Beaty'll have to take me to the hearing centre."

Juliane rose. "You know, auntie, you can always count on me to take you on errands."

"What errands?"

"Drive you to the hearing aid people, to the hospital. Here's my number."

Ivy frowned at Juliane running a hand through her hair spirals and sighed, "Me hair used to look like yours, only dark. Came down to me waist. Some bloke tried to paint me." Her features softened, "I may look decrepit to you but being twenty-odd don't feel so far back."

"Oh auntie, what's so bloody hriveled about twenty-odd? At college there's me in a draughty room with three other girls. Then I'm slaving all hours at the egg plant. Now I'm stuck on the sixth floor with two kids. Opening tins, stumbling over toys, wiping sticky hands, patching up fights and not ten quid to spare. Where are the perqs?"

"You don't seem to have the times we had."

"And I'm not looking forward to forty, let alone eighty. How do you get that old?"

Ivy cleared her throat. "Childhood felt like forever but once married, a month of Sundays rushes in and out like a fast train. I remember me long hair like it's this afternoon. Forget forty. Fifty sneaks up and if you get through cancer or stroke you might see eighty."

•

Hardly had Juliane said ta-ta when Ivy found herself deep in that last night of life before Beaty. The night Ralph went for the midwife, unable to tell the next street, St. Chads Avenue, from Piccadilly. He's under the lamppost trying to read me writing. Counting on his fingers till he made it up to Inhurst Road, hanging on the bell till Vera's kid opens up. Her in nighties and curlers shouting, 'Cheer op! Soon ye'll be holdin' a lov'ly babe. What'll yer be callin' un then? Is it yer first? The last! Cheer op. It'll all come right like ninepence.' All this before he knocks down her hall stand!

He was in a helluva state, holding Sunday papers up to light the fire, coal dust all over the floor, on his knees at my bedside reciting the Lord's Prayer. He must have been praying for a cushy job that would pay better than Cunard. What he got was hours in queues at the Labour Exchange!

We had Vera listening to babe here, there, left, right and centre, querying heartbeat, calling out, Foetus immobile. And finally, "Should we get old Bicknell? Yeh, get the bugger." Hobson's choice. Ralph's out again, up to the corner phone box. Gets through to Casualty and finds out Bicknell's off sick! Dropping my name, he gets another number. Ages later, in comes a baby face who puts an ear to the foetus and gives me a shot. An intense contraction follows on and me screams scare the daylights out of us.

"Now Nurse Gorwick," says Babyface. "Between ourselves, can you remember taking a sedative? Anything at all...No hemming and hawing! I won't tell."

I had to own up. Potassium bromide. There we are in the birth posture: with him and Vera inducing the next contraction, holding forceps to exit. Push, they order, and no sign. Then to forceps insertion. Nothing for ages then after lot of fishing round I dilate, the head slides out and we're home and dry. There's Vera and the intern holding up Ralph! After pelvic stitching, I come round to the red-faced kid wrapped in a hand towel and Ralph managing to bring out coffee and then rushing out to catch the 6.35 AM workman's bus to get Maw.

There's our Maw carrying on something chronic about the state of the flat. Nowhere to put anything. Blood all over the place. No wonder that hubby looked like a corpse. What we have to ask is, "What the bloody hell was our Ive doing giving birth at home? I always wondered about her. Oh at school, she was a favourite! Got commended. Words like "excellence" and "dexterity." But what about sense? Still it's a luverly little thing with its black hair. Yawning and guzzling to beat the band. Though I see its eyes haven't opened! Still, thank the Lord for small mercies: Ive's managing to squeeze out a few drops of milk!

There were times Rosie next door minded baby so we could get out to the Green Post or go indoors for a cup of tea. Maw and Omar still treated Ralphie like a son though he got strange looks when they heard about the dole. He'd applied for temp work as a bartender and finished up as a dustman, getting up at five, working through till one. Slept till three, then did food shopping and got the meals. At the weekend cleaned latrines at the Vernon.

"What kind of a name is Beatrice?" Myrtle wanted to know. "Why not something snazzy like Gloria or Beryl? By the way, Maw, did you know the baby's eyes are blue?"

"What? Oh my God! Why didn't you say? Glory be! How long did that take? Where are we now? February?"

Pop and Ralph had gone out for a walk. Maw and Myrtle were getting the tea. And me by the fire, catching words. About me. Trouble was they read the birth certificate: Father: Ship's Steward, Mercantile Marine! Pop mumbling about cleaning cabins and deck work. "If that's all the bloke's good for, he better try waiting at table." Then Maw: "The ship's putting out to sea, somewhere foreign. Calling at Bermuda, or Madeira was it? Then what? Eh? Laid up again?"

I heard them all talking. "The trouble with our Ive, she don't let on," Myrtle murmuring. "Never has. I asked her why she had it at home, her being an SRN and champion breech birther. And she says: 'Because I did that's why!'"

Never knew why our Maw must take things so seriously, raising her voice, "We all know Ive's a bugger. Always has been."

10 GLEBE REPOSE

The 11.04 gliding out of Waterloo, platform 16, picked up speed a mile on. As it clattered across the rails, a familiar burning took hold of Triss, threatening a flood. Bent double, she hit the facility as the train came to a stealthy halt then jerked forward, swinging the toilet door back to disclose Triss to the swaying carriage.

At the Glebe Repose front hall, a tight-lipped Garcia met Triss at the stairway: Mother had taken hrive barbitone, three times the dose! Pushing open her door revealed the hunched-over figure, hair in tufts, topcoat over pyjamas, croaking, "Where the bloody hell? …You got no consideration!" The room more disordered than ever, and a brand new pot of bulbs on the window sill.

"I get on the bus to Cosham to get tonic wine. Just as I see a seat I'm jerked off me feet. Couldn't get up, so they empty the bus! Next thing I'm at QA and the first thing I hear is I'm a has-been taking up a bed!"

In the noonday light, hriveled and twisted, an abstract version of self, Ivy's voice broke into the chaos: "There's me on me jack. Job's gone. House gone. Nurses don't give a toss. When I try to read there's a slug in the way."

"What about the stiff upper lip?"

"Bugger the stiff upper lip."

"Somebody sent you a pot of bulbs didn't they?"

"Go out and get me some Strepsils. I got a sore throat."

On a traffic island Triss spotted, between vehicles, Uncle Art pushing a shopping cart. Scanning Boots, the Co-op and the optician's, she caught up with him at Dewhurst's, pointing to sausages in the freezer display.

"Look here, lover," Art said, collecting chipolatas in bunches of ten. "The nurse on duty told me your Mum made a big to-do about sling stretchers putting her back out. Consequently it took time to get her settled in the ward an 'at, and the minute I open me own front door, the hospital's on the line to bring in night things and clean underwear.

Then they wait for me to get back to the ward to tell me brushed nylon's too hot. So back I had to traipse to the Glebe to fish out her cotton pyjamas."

"How long was she in?"

"Until I got the call to collect."

"I mean what period in hospital?"

He squinted at the weighing machine. "Ooh, three nights."

"You heard about the overdose?"

"Look, duckie," he poured change into a purse, buried the parcel of sausages in the shopping cart and zipped it up, "we didn't phone because we wanted to help you to avoid taking more time off work."

With Mum sucking on a Strepsil, Triss got her settled with brewed Twinings and an Osborne biscuit. Mopping mother's face with a warm flannel, Triss hesitated then asked after uncle Art's character.

"Character?" Ivy cleared her throat then rubbed one eye, "Cock of the walk! Been like that since he was a nipper."

"How can a nipper be cock of the walk?"

"As a kid he had to have what you had and that was his stock in trade."

"Does he take after Omar?"

"His dad!" Mum frowned, stroking her nose.

Triss poured her a second cup. "Didn't you say Art was a schoolboy when you got married?"

"No. Delivery boy. Why can't you listen? Maw had him at forty-two. Omar showed up after eight years and four weeks out foreign! With him around, her life went back to kitchen sink, soaking pots, scrubbing collars, rinsing and manglin:. Pregnancy, gin, laudanum, scalding baths. Brushes and soap all over the floor! And at the end of it all, there's Boy Arthur! In technicolor! She wasn't half fed up! Shoved him onto me! I had to get up from homework to change him. In fact, her having him cut out my scholarship. Instead of going on to the Sec, I had to stay nearer home and hang out nappies." She removed a tea leaf from her tongue. "Maw had favourites."

"Like who?"

"All the men," Ivy sniffed. "Except took to you."

"Me?"

"I brought you up to be disciplined."

"What kind of discipline?"

"Obedience."

"Ah!"

Musing, Ivy pulled at a hair on her chin. "Maw couldn't have had much time for him because she dint bother with discipline. Our Art can be a pest. His range is small, very small. But," she tapped the table runner, "where money's concerned he's level-headed."

Triss clenched her jaws, "How is a small-range man better with money than a woman?"

"You don't hear him complain of shortages. Doesn't NEVER go around looking half starved." Ivy gulped tea, thrust the cup and saucer back for refill. "Told me that financially speaking I got nothing to worry about."

"If you're not hit by inflation."

"What do you know about inflation?"

"If Glebe Repose increases rents to keep pace with the cost of living, you might find yourself with taxed money that had become cheaper."

"Oh, don't talk such rubbish! If you knew one thing about finance you'd have a few bob behind you. But no, you must scrape along with odd jobs like cat minding. Why you never got on with your life I can't think. It's all to do with identity." Reviving, Ivy sat up as if reviewing a march past.

Triss shouted, "With all the plants, the room's starting to look like a funeral parlour."

Their eyes met. "I get lovely flowers from Juliane; even young Marlina offered to help in between whiles. When you're not here, like."

"Help? With what?"

"Oh maybe odd bits of shopping."

Pale and constrained, Triss stacked crocks.

"Push the mixer tap to the left for the hot."

"When did the younger one show up?"

"Marlina left a gloxinia on the hallstand," mother pulled out a cushion and shook it.

Triss sat lifeless.

"Daydreaming won't get you far."

"When does Juliane come?"

"Now and then," Ivy leant forward. "Drives a car. If I've promised to leave her something, I suppose I'll have to do the same for Marlina. It's only fair." Ivy lay back in the armchair, eyes half closed. "If you must know," she sighed, "I took an overdose."

Triss stared at her nails. If she'd swallowed the right dose her heart could have stopped by now.

11 IVY CAN'T SLEEP

At nine-thirty Ivy put aside her library book and switched off the lamp. The room was now more or less set up, and falling asleep was not automatic. The night was black and moonless. At the window she watched Lila and Aggie handed out of a shiny saloon car by son Brian. She lay watching car lights sweep the ceiling, a lighted replica of the window traversing to a spot on the wall where it swelled to a wide diamond before switching itself out. Streetlight beams shooting through the three lawn conifers made skeletal patterns on the curtains.

Came a vision of Battenburg Avenue, a Sunday morning. Ralph had got up at six and brought in a tray, saying, "Isn't it lovely?" and me hushing him.

"Just being here," he was whispering, "the two of us."

"Three of us now."

"Moments like these," he poured her tea and sat up in bed, "I've been thinking, Ivy." He handed her the cup and saucer. "Thinking."

"Well?"

"About coming out."

"Coming out! Out of Cunard? You're always telling me you love the 'Beri.'"

"So I do."

"Well then."

"It's hard, Ivy."

"With your mates in the pantry?"

"It's the hours."

"I've worked nearly twelve hours meself. Most nights I'd soak me feet."

"My mates take on more hours than that. Up at five-thirty. Put out the first class breakfasts. Cut grapefruit, peel spuds, grill bacon, kippers. Coddling, boiling, scrambling, frying eggs sunny side up, both sides. Turning sausages. Whipping up mash. All from scratch. Special orders. Steak and chips. Salad."

"Sounds like the life for me."

"Cost you a few quid."

"I mean as pantrywoman."

"Pantrywoman! I must put that to Harry. Anyway, when the last rasher gets jerked back and washed down with the last gulp of char, we're clearing the decks for elevenses in the sun lounge. Café au lait, buttered muffins. Gorgonzola, Rocquefort. Setting it out. Giving 'em gout. Clearing away. Till the next *da-hay*."

"Not you alone!"

"No Ivy! The crew! By five minutes to noon we'd be setting up the top deck lunch. A break. Then hors d'oeuvres, cold cuts and fiddly desserts but at least we're not sweating our guts out. After that then what? Four o'clock tea. Finger sandwiches. Patisserie galore. Raspberries and fresh cream."

"They're chomping all day long!"

"Then there's a breather in the pantry. But, if tea folds at 5.15, is *dinnah* far behind? Taking from seven ooh sometimes to midnight. So figure it out for yourself how many hours."

"Not when you're in port, surely to goodness?"

"Big clean up. Inventory checking. Bills for intake. Look Ive, I'm thirty-seven years old. That's when some people die. Famous people. Like Gershwin."

"But you're not famous."

"The fact is: I want to work eight hours a day. Not eighteen."

"Din't they say you're the best carver in the Atlantic?"

"There's one other thing. Don't misunderstand me. I'm devoted to you, always will be. But I'm in need of time for us alone. I've been through a lot and a father's role is not my be-all."

Ivy turned her pillow over. She'd asked Garcia to pull the window down and the silly bitch had slammed it shut. She heaved off the duvet, and squirming around till her feet found the carpet, picked up her spectacles and glanced at the wall clock. Quarter past four. Seeing her library book, *Death of a Caretaker*, she felt around for the reading glass. The clock hands jumped to four-thirty along with the vision of a cup of tea. But there's no more milk. She chewed her lips. Doesn't that housekeeper get up at five?

Fire regulations in place, the swing door felt weighted to Ivy, pushing and panting. Once outside the housekeeper's room, she knocked once, twice, then began pounding, singing out, "Garcia, are you there?"

After a longish interval, a high clucking voice cried, "Who on earth can this be?"

"Me. Mrs. Gorwick."

"And what do you need?"

"I wonder if you could oblige me with a little milk?"

An interval then, "Look, Mrs. Gorwick, I wish you'd go back to sleep."

"Eh?" Ivy adjusted her hearing aid.

"If you don't mind, go back to sleep."

Mumbling "Bugger and shit," Ivy did a three-point turn back down the passage, put all her weight on the fire door, fumbled for the stair-lift button and in darkness sailed down the wooden ziggurat. In the kitchen, grabbing a kettle, she half-filled it, placed it on the cooker and switched on. Opening the refrigerator, she squinted at milk containers and frowned over skimmed and two per cent.

Her deliberations floated back to the Town Station ticket line en route to a wedding. Ralph in his wedding suit careering around to the ringing train bell, encircling his head with his fists, calling, "Seconds out the ring!" Her in a sage green costume with "het to metch." A few halves of Bass and gin chasers at the railway bar. The ceremony was blacked out.

Fumes coming up, then more smoke. Clanging. Spotting the mangled kettle, she tossed it into the sink where it exploded into flames. Calmly she held it under the cold tap, then sauntered along the passage, fumes following up the stairs.

Clem, the fire monitor, hurried along the corridor, knocked and entered each room, "Ladies, are you decent? I'm making a reccy to see if the staircase is viable. Now please, do not use the stair lift."

"I need your attention, all," cried Ivy. "I may have dealt with it. This section's fireproofed so we'd be better off staying here."

"Are we ready?" Clem called, handing out fire blankets. "Now Ivy, Eve, Hope, Prue, let's proceed downstairs. Yes, Mrs. Hotch, Suzi after me, hold firm to the pussy cat, then Eve and Hope, you Lila, and Aggie.

"Somebody please get hold of Mabel and Hetty." She unlocked the front door and all residents except Ivy picked their way down the asphalt, forming a tight circle at the gates, while Clem scurried back to alert Garcia.

The night had an unseasonable chill and residents, wrapped in fire blankets, drew closer to Prue and the cat, tuning in to intimations of minimal smoke and no more alarm bell, ergo the commonsense of a return to the room. After a few minutes' absorption, one by one they straggled up the drive through the wide open front door.

Having contacted the Fire Station, Clem had made sure doors were closed, then searched the drive, first left to the bus stop and then right as far towards the Red Lion.

The fire engines fetched up with a two-man unit leaping off and running alongside ladders and hoses. Steel-helmeted firefighters stormed passage and stairs, opening doors at random, jolting Aggie, and converging at the open back door where Garcia had flung the plastic kettle onto the lawn. The stove got a good hosing down, flooding kitchen and utility room and soaking the hall carpet.

From an upstairs window, Ivy surveyed the scene.

12 DORITA

Next morning at ten minutes past ten, Jovian Plum swept into the Glebe library. The Chair, Mrs. Hotch, waited till he had smoothed out his papers, to say on a stirring note, "Now that we are all present, I have news. Dorita has been appointed to the Glebe Repose regional board." Amid the "Well well's" and table thumping, Dorita Gitling's rigorous features slackened while the Chair consulted her personal list which had to do as an agenda. 13 May 1992:

Cat flap
Housekeeper's relief time.
Cost of fire cleanup and Ivy Gorwick.

The first items were soon dealt with. At Item 3 the Chair, reaching into her dress to adjust a bra strap, sighed, "Residents absorbing impact of fire alarm in dead of night and no clarification. Dorita Gitling has notes on Ivy Gorwick."

Dorita, hands on table, declared, "My mother's nursing home, the Stellarmount, recalls an instance of preliminary caution served on a *certain employee*," scanning the table. "This, followed by a secondary caution, smoothed the way to *dismissal*."

The Chair raised an eyebrow, "Do I hear a motion?"

Eyes aglow, Plum broke into the concerted buzz with, "Mrs. G. is eighty-five. She disposes of house and home to move into the Glebe. There's removal trauma to consider."

"Trauma!" Dorita snorted. "Does Clem Dollgordon behave like a gremlin? Does Prue Bover?"

Plum fingered a notch on the table. "The Glebe Repose mandate is care and respect."

In the tomblike silence, Reverend Goth raised his head, "I move there be a study period."

The Chair shot a smile at the vicar, "Could you manage a pastoral call?"

The Reverend removed the pencil from his mouth. "Indeed, Fan, I could. Except my mother's just had a fall and I'm having to drive down to Bath this afternoon. Could it wait a few days?"

The Chair gritted her teeth. "Jove, you might want to grab the nettle. Wasn't the woman your admission?"

"Well, Fan, are pastoral calls in line with accounting?"

Dorita raised her eyes. "Residents are making symptomatic noises. About moving."

Jove sighed, "One of us might take the daughter aside."

Garcia's chubby face round the door triggered a tabling as elbows yielded to coffee and crumpets and Jove, catching her eye, murmured, "Do we have data on the Gorwick daughter?" and Garcia's response, "Works in charity. Shades of green."

Under cover of the commotion, Dorita Gitling edged her chair closer to Fanny Hotch. "When he," she murmured, flicking eyes in Plum's direction, "and my brother were chosen as finalists out of forty-four applicants, he," lowering her tone, "was preferred over Nigel, for reasons of...charisma. Does an accountant have a feel for character?" Dorita edged further forward, nose to nose, adding, "We discarded the Gorblimey's application and Plum put her back!"

Fan dropped her shoulders in a sigh. "A test of his interpersonal skills. Any more than is his suitability. I only met his wife the once but I did take to her.""I say his fixation on affordable care has irritated some on the governing board."

"Well, let's bear in mind Chairman Kleindl and Jove are close."

13 OMAR

The following Wednesday, the Glebe front door stood ajar. Deep in reflection on Omar and possible Arab ancestry, Triss toiled up the steep staircase. A pair of white trainers and bow legs returned her to the here and now, with Garcia's breathless "Wondered if you'd care to stay for lunch?"

Triss spun round at the fire door. "Thanks but…I'm a vege addict."

"No sweat," Garcia laughed. "I've been swotting up on lipids and diglycerides. Try to make it."

Ivy, struggling with a frock as Triss pushed open the door, cried, "Yep, everything's fine. The old gal across the passage pops in to get her varicose vein dressing changed and o' course when I need her where the hell is Evie? Sh' used to play *goff*, you know," she added, rocking her head in parody. "Truth is I feel like kicking up me 'eels." Swearing at the hook and eye's failure, she lifted arms for Triss to pull down an outsize T-shirt. "By the way, we had our first death! Do-ins gets up, drops her teacup. Sneezes once. Collapses! We lift her up, spread her out on the settee. I take her pulse but," Ivy's brows shot up, "gone. Not a single rattle."

Triss on the edge of the loveseat, eyes on the carpet, muttered, "Who's Doings?"

"You know. Wotchermacallit, the little biddy."

"Prue?"

"Yep."

"What sort of age?"

"Three months off a hundred."

They sat in the noonday light blinking at motes. "Shame really because I warmed up to old Prue." Ivy took up the reading glass. "When I've finished this page I'll go down."

Triss roused herself. "I'm invited by the housekeeper."

"What are *you* doing sucking up?"

"It isn't a question of sucking up."

"Not much."

Tight and confined on the loveseat, Triss stared at her hands, then stretched. "They wouldn't mind, would they, if I took a mini-shower before lunch? Could you spare a towel?"

It was past one o'clock when Ivy and Triss rounded the hall table and took places in front of the french windows.

At the table, Evie Cash extended a bony hand, "It's nice you can get down to see your mother in the week."

"Yes," Triss mumbled, "Wednesday's my free day."

"I'm grateful she's dressing my ulcer," added Evie.

"I hear your office is in Belgravia," Clem said in a baritone.

"Operates from Paddington," Triss whispered.

Residents mulled this over, helping themselves to pieces of lemon sole and stewed parsnip. Room was being made for a pan of roast potatoes and two salad bowls, one mostly green, the other mostly red.

"Well Ivy, I expect that by now you've found homes for your items?" Clem asked in an indulgent tone.

"If I've told you once I've told you a dozen times."

As Clem passed plates and Garcia scanned a list of Prue's clothes, Ivy blurted, "I got to go out!"

Eyes widened.

"Get down to the Guildhall. See a show."

Lila broke in, "It'll only be head-splitting bedlam, all amplification and no talent."

"Yobbos, half-dressed. With tattoos," Aggie put in.

Ivy's lip protruded, "What about us all going out the Pier?"

Evie fluttered her beringed fingers, "We all have fantasies, Ivy. Potted palms. String ensemble. But like the egg and cress sandwich, gone the way of the late night bus. Two dance floors? No, my dear, slot machines! The Café did stagger on for a bit then had to go fast food. Now it's canned rock from the bandstand, foam cups and plastic spoons. The last one to pack up was that extraordinary palmist, the short-haired lady in the tweed suit."

Lowering a fist on the table, Ivy thundered, "I know you all go places. Where do you get to?"

Evie whispered, "If my grandson didn't drive me to my daughter's, I'd hardly get out. One bus every two hours!"

"A car is everything," Ivy declared.

Evie put out a hand, "O Ivy, remember North End before the motor car? Shops open all hours? The crowds! I never considered drunken sailors outside the Blue Anchor all part of affluence!"

"There's the Theatre Royal." Ivy's voice carried above the dish-stacking as she got up, toppling her chair and, hands in pockets, slouched out of the dining room. Residents' heads shook as Garcia, parting the kitchen blinds, cried out, "Look who's here!"

"You come here," Ivy fumed, "you save on food. Save on bath water. When do you open your purse for Chrissake? It certainly can't be for appearance. When's the last time you washed your hair?"

"I was the disciplined child."

"Not much discipline after fifteen. Out dancing every night in *my* clothes and *my* shoes. Walking the streets at all hours. Disco mad!"

A grim Triss set library book, spectacles and reading glass against the table lamp. Disco was Ivy's code word for sex. That the Facts of Life were never reviewed at home had pretty much convinced Triss that to feel right, sex had to be a dirty secret. Aloud she said, "Perhaps you think you resemble your mother. Who was kind."

Ivy scratched her head. "Kind! Maw? Nothing kind about her. Or Omar! Old Man River! When he came home on leave, we had a crisis on our hands! None of us had a right to be home! He'd bolt the back door so if you're coming in from the WC in the pouring rain you'd wait for him to open up. Mrs. Clegg might let us through but only if she was in the mood."

She wiggled in the armchair, lifting a foot for daughter to remove shoes. "By the time Pop retired from the Marines we'd all got out. Maw couldn't leave the street, so Myrtle moved in with her and that made things worse. Over time Maw worked out a routine. Her in the front room, gets up at five. Him upstairs till eleven. Hearing him move she'd go out. He'd shave, finish his bacon and fried bread, then be off. First stop the Still and West." Ivy stroking her nose, added, "Her back from the shops at noon, cooks the meal, has her laydown. From Martha's, Omar staggers down Lake Road to the Tramway, home by two thirty, takes his dinner off the fire and has his laydown. Come six o'clock he's at the Radical Club for cribbage, finishing up at ten, or eleven in the summer." Ivy sneezed. "That was their day, reg'lar as clockwork."

"He was a drunk then."

"Held his liquor."

"Did you get on with him?"

"Get *on* with him!" Ivy worked her chin round. "Spots me birthday card on the mantelpiece. Finds out I turned fourteen. Goes up to the kids' bedroom takes out me underwear and some of Myrtle's, fills a bag. Slings it out the front door.

"Maw waited up. When he came in they had words. Did they have words! You could have heard the carry-on over in Kilmiston Street. Then I see Maw slide the poker out of the fire. Teeth clenched. Him filling his pipe, patting it down carefully. Well, just as he reaches for his hat, she strikes! He moved fast. Still she'd caught him one. Oho yes!" Ivy removed her hearing aid. "A hefty haematoma, burnt on the edges, took months to go down. We all went about whispering. But worse was the tension. Maw had bruises under both eyes.

"I had plucked up courage to say, 'Pop, you don't really want me walking the streets?' He shuffled round treading on me toes. 'Ive,' he says quietly, 'I want you out.' 'Why me?' I said. 'Look Ive, I want everybody out, and you're next.' And he goes, 'Don't come back here tonight expecting to be let in. Because I'm giving you an order. Get out of my house. There are all kinds of live-in jobs. Be a maid. You're big enough and ugly enough to pay for yourself.'"

Ivy cleared her throat, "Me in the street with me canvas bag! Went up to Kingston Cross, turned right into Chichester Road up to Copnor then Milton. Knocking doors, getting leads, asking in shops. Oh there were jobs all right, but no beds! I staggered down St. Mary's back to Kingston Road, and sat outside the Fish Mart on the step. When the missus came out, she took pity on me and offered to take me on as a skivvy. Lost her son in the war and had a spare room. Me duties were: clean the upstairs, get the breakfasts, keep the kitchen clear. Mop the shop out after closing. I was crying with relief.

"It was when Pop's range went from five pubs down to two, then one, the red tiled place at the corner, that they started bringing him home after hours. One of us would leave him off there the next day. Myrtle would hide his braces and belt. He kept all his teeth even though they were soot coloured. The doc couldn't find a thing wrong with him! I laid him out as a matter of fact." Ivy sighed, "He looked lovely in his coffin!"

14 LUNCH IN GARCIA'S ROOM

Compared with mother's, Garcia's quarters radiated calm. Bed, chest; bare floor gleaming as if newly waxed, and a table with four wooden chairs in one of which was Plum tucking a napkin in his shirt collar. Triss caught her breath.

At table center a large bowl of greens and two Zulu ladles.

"Yes," Garcia was saying, sliding a soup bowl in front of the administrator. "Invited Mr. Plum also, Triss. Hope you don't mind."

Triss seated herself, facing a soup that hinted at butterflies and newly mowed fields.

"I think it must be your mother's eyes," Jovian Plum said in a lifeless way. "Fear of spilling things." His eyes widened.

Triss massaged her neck. "Up to sixty-five mother had twenty-thirty vision. In her third year she was invited by Theatre to assist." She wondered if Garcia would mind congratulations on the soup.

"Ah, soda water," remarked Jove. Unlocking his hands, he inquired after Ivy's overdose.

Eyes down, Triss mumbled, "It's not her sort of thing."

Chewing his lower lip, Plum studied Triss's Ivylike nose. "It may be true Ms. Gorwick-Beatrice-that certain semi-active folk, glued to garden, dog and locality, look on retirement homes as a form of storage."

"The market's hardly likely to let you down."

"Does she conform?"

"Mum can be a stickler for conformity," Triss sighed, sampling a fresh spinach leaf, "with phrases like, 'We're ordinary people.' Don't think I'm trying to infer she's commonplace."

"Does she try?"

Triss, stifling a laugh, looked away.

He blinked once or twice. *"As a way to fit in?"*

Triss, emptying her mouth, considered dropped aitches and one verb for all cases while Jove, closing his eyes to phrase a question, finally came out with, "How does Ivy react to central authority?"

"Our local candidate couldn't convince her of the utility of nuclear power."

"I have a knack of summing people up. But in your mother's case I'm getting more than one image."

15 DORITA AGAIN

"I'm sorry to disturb you, Mrs. Gorwick, but I understand you were enquiring about a bath." A week had passed.

Dropping a sponge, Ivy, naked to the waist, grabbed a towel as the stranger tapped her shoulder.

"A bath you say? What about it?"

"Would you like to have that bath now?"

"I might. Instead of the shower."

"Well then," said the visitor with firm kindness, "collect your things and we'll run the water."

"Eh?"

"Just bring bathrobe and soap," added Dorita Gitling, on the short side and muscular, radiating starch and competence.

In a clover bathrobe, clutching a cake of lavender soap, Ivy opened her door, looking both ways. Dorita, bending over the tap, ran fingers through the bathwater. "Now, hold the hoist and lean on me. Lift your right leg."

"I'll have you know I've been bathing patients for fifty years."

"Good, now lift the other leg. Don't let go of the hoist."

"It won't ackle."

"Then hold on to me."

"But this water's lukewarm!"

 Dorita turned on the hot tap, swirling the water about.

"Christ, now it's too bloody hot."

"You won't want to sit down in your bathrobe."

"I don't think I can sit."

"Hold on to me with both hands and ease yourself down."

"It hurts me back."

"Sister Gorwick, it will be hard to soap you down in a bathrobe so take your arms out." Dorita leaned forward to switch on the overhead shower, adjusted the temperature with care. "Test the shower. Is it too hot?"

"No."

"Is it too cool?"

"No."

"Then it's just right."

"Of course it's just right!"

"So pass me the robe and back under the shower."

"I won't."

"Here's a shower cap for you."

"I'm not getting under any shower."

"Come along now. Have a bash." Standing well back, untying the robe, Dorita urged Ivy under the showerhead and, warning her to keep her head away, flicked the robe off, turned on the jet and began soaping Ivy's marble shoulders.

"Give me back my robe you bloody ignorant bitch," Ivy roared. "This is no bath. I order you to stop. At once. I know what your game is. You're trying to drown me."

Panting over the bath rim, the former assistant matron faced the former ward sister of four orthopedic wards.

16 DINNER WITH PLUM

"Well, hell-o Beatrice!" Jovian Plum, under the balustrade, beamed as Triss, with an armful of library books, descended one stair at a time, "I was wondering if ah you might be free for a bit of a chat, if we could manage to set a time?" He sniffed, "Up to when will mother be needing you?"

Triss groped for calm, adopting the half-hearted tone taught at voice class to render an impassioned song, then sighed, "Four o'clock tea."

"If you'd agree to take a later fast train, I would drop you at the station." He stood passive as she calculated how to reschedule the three-dog walk. "Need to consult about a couple of items."

Triss gripped the banister, swallowed hard, gulped.

"Four-thirty in the Methodist car park then?"

At four-fifteen, Triss, in mother's WC, scrubbed nails, teased front hair, and confined the back in a manageable wad. Then, with spritz of scent-free cologne, dash of non-animal pearly lipstick, lacquered eyelashes and nose covered in intelligent cream, she prised hair from sweater and jeans.

"Looks like you're going somewhere," mother commented.

"Well," daughter mumbled, "I ought to be pushing off."

At 4.45 Triss sidled down the Glebe driveway. Jovian Plum at the church parking lot down the road, flung two arms overhead, a Wagnerian conductor in a Lazarus suit. Once slotted into the Jaguar's moulded seat, she composed herself to meet the CEO world of padded leather, sniffing her sleeves, willing away any hint of the Colonel, whom she judged incompletely neutered despite the vet's ruling out of any such grade. Head erect, she inserted a thumbnail under each fingertip.

"Ms. Gorwick-Beatrice-let me reassure you the present situation is no red light. The Glebe Repose mandate is care and respect. Elders are our bread and butter."

Triss rolled her neck on the Jaguar's headrest. "With Battle of Britain overhead, Mum bicycled every night to the hospital where she worked. In blackout with only a dim blue light."

Under Plum's handling and remote from sound of lorries, she relaxed. It was only when the car slid into a hotel parking lot that tension intruded. Trying to stay in the moment, she tailed Plum through the immense lobby, praying to the All that bomber jackets shredded down the front, concertina pants and beat-up track shoes were IN. At the restaurant's glassed-in area, Plum tapped his chin, then settled on a table facing a mini rock garden.

"Peppermint tea," she told the waiter.

"Bit on the late side," Plum suggested. "Would we like a drink?"

"Tap water. No straw and no ice. And no paper napkin."

"Soda water," added Jove.

Plum chewed his lower lip as he threw open the menu, "I might have a little something to munch on. Would you care to join me?"

"I won't say no."

"You don't smoke by any chance?"

"Not since I was fourteen."

With a half grin he signalled to the wine waiter. "A bottle of claret. The '88." He leant forward, "It must be well past five. When is your suppertime?"

"Three times a week I get supper at work, but the other nights...get home by six, feed the cats, clear litter boxes, mop the bathroom, walk the dogs, and sit down, it could be half past ten."

"Your cats. Do they have names?"

She frowned at the rock garden's threadlike waterfall, "Leonetta, Elijah, Piper."

"Umm. On the subject of felines, there's a situation..." Plum murmured.

He must be going on sixty-five.

"I'm told the salad bar has a five-star rating."

"I try to stay off salad at night."

"Join me in a glass o' claret even if it's last year's plonk with a ritzy label." A variable was creeping in. Fire alarm along the London Road.

"Ah, surprise surprise, they've got the '88!" he announced, sampling the *grand vin*. "I'll take my chances on the Mushroom Stroganoff."

She stared at his mouth dipping down one side as he coaxed butter out of a plastic capsule. Then, without warning he flung the butter pat holder over his shoulder. "Fed up with plastic doodads," he explained with a gold-tinged smile." Won't you cast an eye over the hot buffet?"

Entranced, Triss stared at the waiter bending down to retrieve the butter capsule until Plum made a shovelling signal. As she dallied at the illuminated counter, Plum, a morose mandarin, turned to his problem of Dorita Gitling's succession to the regional board.

On Triss's return he said, "Now!" conviviality yielding place to brass tacks.

Flattening the stir-fry, she pondered how to abandon moorings and stay in the shallows. Jove, closing his eyes to phrase a question, finally came out with, "Seizing the Ivy is not easy."

Finding the vintage wine had no harsh undertow, she emptied the glass.

The accountant, chewing slowly, gazed at what looked like a funeral party getting seated.

"As the only one in her class to pass eleven-plus, Mum's brains got ignored at home," Triss told Plum who, watching brown rice and tofu disappear, enquired about her father.

"If she was two minutes late, Dad would take up his place at the window."

"One cannoli, one custard tart and coffee for two."

Plum sat back, sighing, "Being an advocate of the elder voice, I stand by them. But our situation has to be made clear. 'Ivy,' I told her, 'I'm having to take away your hotplate. And after supper the kitchen will be out of bounds.'" The waiter poured coffee and Plum picked his teeth, swooshing soda water. "Tell me," he said, "does she usually comport herself in the military style?"

"Has been called the Sergeant."

"Seems modest."

Triss chewed on filo pastry. "If she'd joined up at the outbreak, she might well have entered as lieutenant."

Plum fanned out his credit cards. "How about Ivy the General?"

Triss started to laugh, coughing into her napkin.

17 DELIE

In response to news of the dispersion of Aunt Romola's effects following her death, Triss hastened to Delie's flat where tweeds, hats, costumes, evening wear, ski gear and beads lay on tables, chairs and the vacuumed carpet. Crawling about, Triss pounced on a skirt of sequined black crepe, held it up in the mirror bringing on fantasies of a filmy top, and a need to find one.

"Bob's your auntie," croaked the parrot.

Fumbling for a piece of dried fruit, Delia muttered, "Don't tell me you've run into some old herbert at that Home?"

Studying a few lines on her cheek, Triss sighed, "Before Mum moved to Glebe Repose, I'd have been lucky to get a kind word from the milkman!"

"What is he, a married traveller in carpet cleaners?"

"Administrator and triple A winner of the Golden Age Audit Award. Married."

"Oh I say! *Prospectivo obscuro.*"

Holding a hand mirror, Triss bundled up her hair, sighed again, "Claims to believe," checking angles in another mirror, "in female power to draw autistic male leaders back from the brink!"

They unrolled the blown-up photograph of a stack of euthanized cats with the caption: *Forgo Delay! Spay Neuter Today!*, tugged the sheet taut, and sashayed round for folding. Delie, glancing at her mother's wristwatch, said, "We'll just have to catch them up at Parliament Square."

"Asked about my cats," Triss mumbled.

Delie bent over to fit the banner into a sackcloth bag, Maya back on her head. "No!" she exclaimed. "Truly, where do you think you'll sport this see-through drapery?"

Triss folded the shimmering pile, "It's the Glebe's annual dinner. The least I can do for Mum is keep my end up."

18 THE GENERAL

Safety pin in mouth, Ivy tightened the elastic stocking, pulled and fastened; Evie sighed in contentment.

Returning to her room, rerolling a stray curl, Ivy announced to her daughter, "Relief housekeeper's laying on a spread for Clem's birthday. Slap-up meal. It's members only so it's no good you getting tidied up." Lurching about the room and eventually out the door, mother left Triss cocking an ear for the chair lift click. A pot of amaryllis whose shades of mauve blocked Triss's thinking till she saw the florist's card: 'Never Out of Our Thoughts, Artie.'

Not too long later, Ivy, head lowered, burst into the room. "Horsy lot of old duchesses. But *tirribly khaind*! Spuds half roasted, scutty bit of turkey, ham lounced out like it's wartime. Marge done up as butter. But I know different!"

"Is anything up, Mum?"

"Plenty."

"Such as?"

Ivy wrestled with her hearing aid, stamped her feet. "You and Joe Plum talking about me behind my back!"

"Did Brother Art suggest that?"

She pointed a finger. "You keep him out of it! Why wasn't I there, I'd like to know?"

"Give JP a call and find out."

"Did that very thing," Ivy scratched the back of her neck. "Couldn't get any sense out of the bloke. Going on about *minoosha*." She wrinkled her eyes, and sighed. "It's not right. Don't kid yourself you got any chance of hooking up with likes of the Plums. They're more respectable than you. With your knees coming out of your jeans and your dreadlocks." Feet astride, a hunched-up

Ivy faced the window, surveying the car park. A car door slammed and she did a quarter turn. The shape of mother in silhouette made Triss let go of the *Daily Scope* and hold her breath. Against the waning sunlight, nose pointing down, hands behind back, Triss espied the General!.

The air in the room stiffened with Triss, now staring at the *Daily Scope*, willing mother to go down to tea. At 4.32 she glanced up and said, "This paper's loaded with nothing but battles and minefields."

"Warfare is man's expedient," Mum replied with a stare.

"Men in helmets holding burp guns. Riding around in armoured cars! Excited about rocket launchers. No sane woman would find herself in that kind of spiel except by default."

"It's men's role in life. Keeps the numbers down."

"Bombing and strafing?"

"Defense! So you can go to bed at night and not worry about the enemy at the back gate with a machine gun giving you five minutes to take your stuff and quit. Can't you get that through your head?"

"Who's the enemy?"

"Could be the next door neighbour." Stroking her nose, Ivy continued, "Me own memory of the Thirties was a civilized sort of time. But apart from the Depression there were Japs in China, Mussolini in Tripolitania. I remember saving up for a winter coat in a Belmont sale and feeling satisfied! Until I spotted a column in the paper about millions in the Ukraine dying of starvation!"

A glum Triss peeping at the giant clock muttered, "What would you say to a course in conversational French?"

"French!" Her mother turned down both sides of her mouth, "English is good enough for me."

"Would you be keen on a Mediterranean cruise one of these fine days?"

"I might," replied mother, in a military nod.

"Some cruise ships make a stop at Corsica." Triss moved her chair closer. "They say it's still picturesque."

"Probably no better than Clacton."

"There's always St. Helena," Triss added, noting mother's eye movements. "I doubt that's seen much in the way of change."

"Who's St. Helena?"

Triss spoke slowly and distinctly: "An island off the east coast of Africa, in the lower Atlantic."

"You don't half have some strange ideas."

As they parted at the top of the stairs, mother declared, "I know what's in your head. Cruising around the Mediterranean, all exes paid, pointing out the beauty spots!"

19 HARBOUR VIEW INN

Hugging the wall, Triss, in her polar coat with the hood up, crept down the drive, turned in a direction opposite to where she was going, crossed the main road at a distant point, and darted up a quiet lane to emerge at the south exit of the Methodist car park. Plum, with a half-grin, swung round, holding the car door open. Settling into the saloon's ambience she watched the waxy hands steer them into traffic.

"How is the Chief of Staff doing?" he asked as they slowed for the stop light.

Triss shrugged, "Concerned about a neighbour at the back door with a burp gun." He joined her in a quiet laugh.

At the traffic lights he sighed, "How will the General spend her birthday? With you?"

"It was in March."

"Ah. And yours? I may have them confused."

"Yes. Mine is due and I'll be here at the Glebe party."

"Ah. The General does not venture to the capital."

"Trains and taxis bring on nausea."

"Does her brother invite her?"

"Never."

At the Harbour View Inn, Plum found the same table and pulled out the selfsame chair for Triss. Pondering the meeting's *raison d'être*, she crossed her fingers. As the waiter handed out menus, she got the nod. Plum stared after her loping over to the hot plate, noting the half-starved look: bony shoulder, capable hands, rarely giving attention to self? That face has style. Skull contours around the eyes, for instance, does bid fair to beauty! From behind a medium portion of pasta *al pesto*, he watched her scraping up tofu and coconut.

Chewing slowly, Triss was sorting through memorable Yuletides. Age fifteen. Parents flat out on either side of dying fire, aroused by rat-tat. Youth outside, red nose and hands. Hiked six miles with silk handkerchiefs! Mum hissing words like "lout" and "yobbo."

Age eighteen. Dad clattering downstairs, hurls Mum's untouched festive tray at the kitchen window, a sight never forgotten by Mrs. Pratt.

Family gatherings at Gunner Street for annual Xmas club share-out. Maw ladling punch with Ralph's guiding hand. Myrtle emptying Maw's medicinal brandy into her own glass; fervent voices melding in "Jezebel."

"Mum used to bring dozen mince pies," Triss said at length, pushing coconut around in tamari, recalling Dad's throat pulsating under his tankard. Bus home crowded, passengers clinging onto rail, roaring and ogling. Driver seeking out Request Stop in the dark. Mum floundering. Dad face down in the snow, nothing to do with drink. Triss bedded down with cat, lulled to sleep by retch and toilet flush.

Jove stirring fusilli, "To take the edge off of debility," he put down his fork, "might the General be amenable to having a puss?"

"What?"

"Obviously our board are not in favour of sheltering any felines. We weren't clear whether mother might have kept a puss."

"Three in toto. Put down before their time. One of my earliest memories is of a drowning."

Jove held the napkin to his mouth.

"Grey water butt next to the rose bush. Female, brown tabby."

Several long moments blanked out ambient sounds until Plum lifted his elbows and asked after her charges.

"Two in street recovery. One with suspected peritonitis." She picked at her nails, "Cats have their dreams. An unattached person with references."

Nodding for a spot more coffee, he said, "Tell me, do you ever smile?"

"What is there to smile at?"

"Just then you looked strangely photogenic; there's beauty around your eyes."

She felt a hot flush come on.

From between his credit cards, Plum abstracted a nose shot of a shorthaired tuxedo cat: "Rory: Found by a nephew in a Derry street. Cowering in my wardrobe. Not my nephew, the cat. The late Prue Bover had kindly agreed to help out."

Triss put the photo down. "I've got four like him."

"My nephew travels to war zones and my sister's allergic." Excusing himself, he waded over to the green-flounced dessert table to idle at the array of cheesecakes. Returning empty-handed, he added, "Rory would come with food, wet and dry. Moderate vet fees recouped. Catnip."

An air of grim authority came over Triss. "Few outside my ministry have a clue about cat survival let alone cat psychology. Two of mine, Falstaff and Valentino, found in maggots in an empty flat. Tenant evicted for arrears. Both fed through tubes," she sucked on a tooth. "My function is preparation for a caring home. But," she bit her lip, "too often has Muggins traipsed miles with cat carriers and got soaked to the skin at deserted bus stops, all to have kitties returned with excuses like: 'My boyfriend! My baby! We're moving!'" She lifted the wineglass and drained it.

"Allergies?" widening gray eyes. "Don't make me laugh! No, Mr. Plum, sadly I must decline. Because, in strictest confidence, my complement is over the top."

"Rory is not any cat," Jove said quietly.

"If I hear that again I'll scream."

"Would you at least agree to a viewing?" He got up, edged over to the dessert counter, did a smart about turn and returned.

Triss sighed, "This evening has to be ruled out."

"Unless you'd be prepared to spend the night."

Triss raised her eyebrows. The night! Abandon feeding time and dog walks for a bewitching discussion at the five star hotel? She sipped from the refilled wineglass. Starting out with puss and sliding into a discussion of past partners and AIDS.

"Were you ever married?"

"Waiting for parents outside a pub, a drunken matelot ogled me, making me feel like a rare orchid. I was thirteen. Years later after most of my pals had got matched, I made a study of the married state *vis-à-vis* coiffure, couture and cocktails and discovered all is a decoy. An Astarte-type goddess meta-morphoses into a drudge, trying to balance working days with sleepless nights. Wives taking any kind of hackwork to escape the mess. And come home to it."

"How old are you now?"

"Fifty-six," she said defiantly.

"And marriage the safe harbour?"

"Bills paid on time might make it tolerable. But from what I don't hear, it seems that satisfactory married sex is not the norm. I wonder about actors writhing about on film to entertain the cameramen. Married friends won't touch the subject. My own contention is: the male organ has x times more sensation than the vagina."

Speechless he sat as she went on, "Take me. Rock exploring in Cornwall with a lad I met on the tour bus. Wife and kids at the beach. After an hour or so of climbing I got out of breath. Seeing me stretched out in a hollow in the cliff must have read like a call to dalliance. Rain was coming on and..."

"And?"

"He fussed around making me comfortable and one thing led to another. I admit the run-up was passable. Until penetration which I recall as bumpy. Next thing, there's commotion nearby that brought the whole business to a halt. A motor boat with a pair of louts in yellow oilskins waving binoculars! Ergo, for many years, I've pretty much stayed out of the arena."

Plum sat for a while then, rousing himself, murmured, "You never were in love?"

"Ah well, there's the dark night and pressure on the bed, and a person with cold feet nestles down beside me, gradually warming up. Bliss! Whether it's skinny little Piper with the loud purr, or the Colonel who must get closer!"

She made a fanning sign, and Plum, frowning and blinking, got up and lurched over to the cheese board.

On return he said, "What I meant, Beatrice, was that Glebe Repose has a guest room for visitors in the event of, ah, certain predicaments."

"I must admit," he exclaimed, to a shrivelled Triss trailing behind, "you do hold your own against the vine! I'm wondering, if you could, or wouldn't mind, taking the wheel?"

She blew her nose. "The last thing in the world I'm capable of."

"I wouldn't...ah...suggest it, except I just...don't feel right. Need to get a breath of sea air."

Dismayed by the dashboard gadgetry, she sat, eyes closed, calling on the All, then taking deep breaths, turned the ignition key, shakily guiding the car across the asphalt where, poised before the line of traffic and, peering left, right, behind, and under the mirror, she broke into the fast lane, flying past giant road signs illuminating names of childhood haunts.

At the Milton exit he decided that, for one who derides autos, her handling is actually not bad. Does her haphazard lifestyle, he began to wonder, conceal a different trajectory?

Approaching Ivy country, Triss passed within sight of the Hospital, whizzed down St. Mary's Road, past the cemetery, braked at mother's old school rebuilt, and turned right instead of left at Kingston Church. This skirted the fault line between nostalgic and new, unsettling, like the medical centre on mounds of green where Maw and Omar's street used to be. Then left into Kingston Crescent past the former site of Daley's School. Still at prayer, she entered the former Mile End Road, now a highway. At the town station, veering left, following Plum's directions through Landport Terrace, she skirted the Ladies' Mile, Rock Garden Pavilion and, eventually, the Pier. A street lamp throwing exotic shadows around a coppiced ash tree led to a street of l920s villas and the beach.

Head spinning, Plum stirred. "I'm ...indebted," he managed to say. "Must take a turn on the beach."

She got out, slapped the car key on the bonnet and squinted at the rail timetable. It was a sweet June night, silent but for the sea's hiss.

"That's our place," Plum told her, scooping up the key, jerking a thumb towards a yellow villa, then staggered across the main road to the promenade and, from a flight of steps, beckoned. The air felt soft, pure even. As they stumbled over pebbles to a belt of damp sand, a shadow low to the ground darted out from under the sea wall. "Shhh," Plum whispered, "the vixen. Luckily I kept a bit of Brie. No, my God! It's Rory!" The lean, black Bombay with a white patch gobbled the cheese, made one leap and clambered up his suit to "Mandy forgot to let you in, didn't she?" On a beach groin, they rested, nudging the cat, scratching his receding brow and behind his tiny ears. Plum, lamenting the perils of crossing a thoroughfare, put out an arm enclosing the cat and Triss. There they sat staring at the near full moon reflected on the dark tide.

Strange. Not exactly warm or tender. He hasn't made a pass. He's here for me because he's like me! All the warmth I need with Rory's gentle purr. I ought to pull myself together, get to the station. Must not miss the train. But now he's talking to the cat! Plum struggled to his feet and singing, *Là ci darem la mano,* Rory draped around his neck, he fed her lines. Her voice came out clear and shaky. A pair of youths, loitering on the prom, mouths full of pizza, started to cheer.

20 ANNUAL GLEBE DINNER

"She thrashes around," Aggie was saying, "like a ruffian!"

Hope declared, "Holds her spoon like a shovel. Can't even speak the Queen's English.

"Never heard of civility. Some thugs come in black leather and spikes. This one's in a pinafore dress."

"Concussed from the parachute jumps," Clem put in kindly, "and, you know, many thugs are actually buffoons at heart. Perhaps we oughtn't fall into the trap of taking her seriously." Three other ladies at the library table frowned at wooden letter chips.

"When that washing machine stopped," Aggie piped, "she reckoned I wasn't mechanical. Does she think I don't know how to push buttons?"

"I never want to see those frosty eyes again," said Lila.

"Like Prue, she could drop dead," added Clem.

"You can't count on these things."

"It's a wonder the daughter shows up."

"With a Ma like Gorblimey I'd have set m'sights on New Zealand… That's eleven, trebled." Hope's brow cleared.

"I hear your house may become available," Lila said to Hope.

"My star tenant had a job transfer. Paid on the dot. Scrupulous," she sneezed. "I've spoken to the Home Help office…No, can't go. No vowels…It's a four-bed, two-bath detached. TV room, Sunroom. Shrubbery. Finished basement. I say, the two of you wouldn't care to move in with me?"

Lila and Aggie looking at each other, chorused, "We had thought of it."

The rattle and thump of preparation yielded place to the combo tune-up. A husky laugh, floating aloft, held its own in the gallery then sank into the buzz of conviviality where Ivy in black velvet and Triss in sparkling skirt and translucent top were announced at the door. Tables with silverware were set under mini-candelabra and an immense No

Smoking sign. In the gallery, the Reverend Goth at the piano and two gaunt ladies on accordion and drum, struck up a set from 'The Desert Song.'

Evie, hanging over Ivy, hollered above *Then You'll Know*, "Prue Bover's daughter also popped off."

"Go on!" Ivy exclaimed, readjusting her top teeth. "She must be pushing seventy!"

"Turned eighty-two!"

"Well, I'm buggered!"

When a tablecloth and comestibles began to show, the band seized its chance for a break and Rev. Goth strolled back from the *ad hoc* bar clutching a tray with two gin and tonics and a horse's neck. Convinced the china was plastic look-alike, Triss went to confirm and, glowing, passed a Crown Derby plate to Ivy, filling her own with stir fry and sauce béchamel.

Garcia, standing behind Plum, lifted up a shocking pink peignoir, sales ticket dangling, with "Here we have a brand-new line! Never been on a woman's front."

As the last item was bid, Triss joined the queue to pay for Ivy's trivet and heard Plum, just behind, describing Rory's need of company. After dessert, she quitted mother's table and slid out to Prue Bover's former room. She hzad begged Plum not to tell Goth it was her birthday and he had complied.

Lolling on Prue's armchair, the mini-panther leapt from ottoman to futon to shoulder. "Nobody knows his age," Plum confessed. "But the older the cat the shorter the commitment. Prue has seen to his every need. Still," he sniffed, "nary a soul has come forward."

An edge in her voice, Triss asked about provision in Prue's Will.

"No mention. But I have acquainted the sole remaining relative with what I believe to be her great-aunt's wish." He stared at Triss's costume with some reserve, allowing that with a chalky complexion, burnt orange and black just might work.

Searching his amber eyes, they opined that Rory might be more of an indoor companion than outdoor predator. In confirmation, the cat lightly jumped over to Triss's lap, climbed her chiffon shoulder, keeping his claws in, and carefully wound himself around her neck and there reclined until Triss nodded okay.

How long they had been sitting there was unclear until loud knocking made the cat jump. A larger-than-life Garcia, hand on chest, pushed open the door, looking around with overbright eyes. "Triss! Mother's here. It's well past ten."

Out in the passage Ivy was hollering, "Where the bloody hell were you? Don't you know they're closing the place up?"

Triss, perched on a bentwood chair, stared at the polished floor, until Jove, announcing the taxi's arrival, slipped her an envelope.

"What do you want the taxi for?"

"Look, Mum, I came dressed for an evening party."

"But you didn't *come* in a taxi!"

21 CATS

"Up to now," Delie commented as they ascended three flights of stairs, "my regard for cats has not been my be-all and end-all. Until I saw your Rory jump."

"I think this must be Ashbury Terrace. Now here we are at flat 16B," Triss sighed. "All they said was Mrs. Lodell was found dead."

They set down carriers and Triss brought out keys trying one after another until the door gave. "Pooh," she cried, holding her nose and rushing across the room to pull down the pair of sash windows. "What have we got here? Hello, little fellow! Oh, sweetheart, you're so bony. And who's this?"

"There are two dead ones in the kitchen."

"Right. We'd better make a count. They told me five." She ran into a smaller room then to the bathroom. "No, there were six, two alive and four dead."

"No, this one's has just opened his eyes."

Triss brought out a china bowl, filled it with water and put it down for two emaciated tabbies. Hobbling about, mumbling, "Thank God," she brought out a small syringe and sprinkled water around the mouth of the exhausted gray.

Delie, making sure the three other cats were stiff, put on humongous gloves, laid each body on newspaper and wrapped it up. One was no trouble, long and flat, the other two, frozen in sitting postures, were harder to wrap and fit into the wooden box they had brought.

Triss worked on reviving the collapsed one, moistening the tongue until finally she saw gulping. She then checked as far as possible for ear mites and maggots, and took out a tin of baby catfood. They each spooned a little into the two cats that could stand. They then wrapped and settled them in the carrier with the wool floor. The third cat they placed on a towel and small blanket and laid in an open basket.

Once outside, Delie asked, "What is today?"

22 CRISIS

On Wednesday, July 15, Triss found mother's door jammed, a magazine wedged under. Pulling and pushing, on hands and knees, she managed to pry the door open. Belts, boots, skirts and corsets were scattered on the floor along with open books. Ivy was hurling shoes across the room.

Triss bent down to right the table lamp.

"Oh no you don't," Ivy screamed, knocking the lamp down.

"Stop it!" Triss panted, grabbing mother by the shoulders. "Sit down."

"Don't you tell me what to do," a loud burst of sobs. "All me life I've been victimized. You'd never believe the sort of scum I've had to work with. Twice matron summoned me to give an account of myself. Them taking home sides of ham! Medicines. And me holding tight to the keys!"

"Mum, what is going on here?"

Through the sobs and the moaning, Triss made out the words "Thrown out."

"Thrown out? You?"

Ivy mopped her face. "The house committee wrote a letter."

"Where's the letter?"

Her mother kicked the mess on the floor. "You find it."

Triss, squatting, rooted through a pile of paper. "What does it say?"

"You ask the daftest questions. I've got a month to clear out."

"I want you to fight this," Ivy shouted from the top of the stairs. "Prepare an address to the board. Circulate petitions. Call the radio station. Don't stand there looking spare. Get on the case."

On her way out to the mobile library, Triss, creeping past the hall table, saw an envelope addressed to herself, marked "Personal for information."

> Ms. Beatrice Gorwick,
> We have today served one month's Notice to Quit
> on your mother Mrs. Ivy Maude Gorwick in accordance
> with Glebe Repose regulation 4(c).

Yours faithfully,
Signed
Jovian Plum, Administrator

"Are you Mrs. Hotch? I'm Beatrice Gorwick, Ivy's daughter. The reason I'm calling is…I'd like to attend the next house committee meeting, if I may."

"Oh yes," came the kind voice.

"I'd appreciate being put on the agenda."

"It's not the committee's practice to include residents or their relatives."

"Even though it may relate to a resident's eviction."

Silence.

"It's hardly standard practice, is it?" Triss stammered.

"I beg your pardon."

"I mean, it doesn't seem democratic."

She heard a sigh, "Ms. Gorwick, this is the way things are done everywhere."

"There must be some by-law setting out exceptions where…where a resident's case can be discussed with a board member."

"Perhaps I might answer your query."

Triss raised her tone. "My question is why?"

"Your mother knocked Aggie Pont down in the utility room. Demanded the housekeeper serve tea in the middle of the night. Subjected more than one resident to verbal abuse. Entered the dining room in raincoat over nightgown. Set off the fire alarm in the middle of the night. Mrs. Bover died two days later."

"Well?" Ivy looked up from her writing pad.

"I ran into rationalizations twenty feet tall."

"You're hopeless! Can't even phone the *Daily Scope!*"

In the doctor's crowded surgery, Ivy, picking at her nails, shouted, "I don't suppose old Cardross could give a damn."

The recycling depot had agreed to Triss's plea for a day off at half pay but could not run to a return rail ticket. The dog walker network complained of being short-changed with Fitz and hinted at permanent replacement; plus Fitz had unilaterally introduced another street cat. Triss felt pressure above the right eye, signalling incoming headache, and wondered about consulting the doctor herself. The buzzer squawked, flashing their number. She helped mother to her feet, and they shuffled into the surgery.

"Jack Spratt could eat no fat," said the doctor. "Which one is here to see me?"

"Me of course," said Ivy.

"Penny for them," Cardross winked at Triss.

"I've been chucked out of Glebe Repose."

The doctor swivelled his chair round. Lowering his spectacles, he shot Triss a sympathetic glance. "How are you weathering it, Ivy?"

"I'm not."

"When is the last time you had a poo?"

"I dint come for that."

"What we're in need of is advice on an alternative residence," Triss said.

"You stay out of it."

"It *is* your Mum, is it?" he flicked the Rolodex. "Have you looked into the George VI?"

"Where Dorita Gittings' mother finished up? Not on your nelly."

"Dorita's mother is hardly Dorita."

"I'm not going to the George."

"The Stellarmount?" Cardross continued, pencil between teeth.

"That hole's overpriced. Worked there fifteen years. Got a lounge like a postage stamp!"

"Twenty-four-hour service. Twice-monthly outings. We'll put that to one side. The Greenray we'd better pass over. There's the Mackintosh! Two communal rooms. View over the downs. Social worker on premises. Library," He turned the card over, "Reasonable!"

"Only five miles from the shops."

The doctor folded his arms, "In your place Ivy, I'd pen a tactful note to each committee member. They meet," he checked his calendar, "Wednesdays. Three o'clock sharp."

"He is helpful," Triss remarked, squinting in the bright December sun.

"Helpful! Talked your father into psychotherapy and after that I had contradiction right up to the end."

23 GLEBE BOARD MEETING

At 3.15 PM on the day of the August Board meeting, Ivy, disdaining the chair lift, hobbled downstairs. Reaching the library and hum of voices, she straightened up, marched to the door, turned up her hearing aid, and, open-mouthed, overheard her name. With clenched jaw and lowered head, she staggered up and down then, ear to the door, knocked inaudibly. Another knock, also light, got no response. She listened in for a moment or two then turned the knob.

"I'm sorry," she began, quaking slightly, as she broke into the committee's line of talk, "but there's something I want to say."

Discussion tailed off. "Ah, Ivy," Jovian Plum rose. "We'll be through in two shakes so if you wouldn't mind waiting, I'll be out to sit with you and answer any points."

"Points. Have I got points?" Ivy, raising her eyebrows, rolled her shoulders and turned her body round. "Yes, I suppose I have." Big smile. "I hope you'll pardon me if I raise one now. How is it that I am being evicted from these premises by letter? No, that's not how I want to phrase it." She put a hand to her head.

Mrs. Hotch said, on a note of regret, "You're not on today's agenda."

"But you're discussing my case!"

The vice chair nodded an I-told-you-so at the chair.

Under the spotlight Ivy bent over, working her jaw, "If you hadn't been discussing me I might have decided to wait but..."

"Mrs. Gorwick, we're holding a meeting," Dorita Gittings thundered.

"...I heard me name come up," Ivy, majestic, eyed each committee member. "If I'm on your agenda you can't justify any discussion of eviction without consultation with me. Eviction as a first resort is unthinkable without advance warning, and more than that, I, Ivy Gorwick, was not approached. Jovian Plum spoke with my daughter! Relegated me to a state of mental incompetence." Hands behind back, she lowered her head, "I sense a form of abuse in your method." Astride and, bending one knee, she shifted weight back and forth. "In my preliminary conversations with Plum, he referred to some kind of Glebe mandate to treat the elders with dignity. My debility was, if I'm not mistaken, interpreted as a symptom of feeble-mindedness. But even were it a correct diagnosis, the procedure would still have violated the mandate."

There was a long pause while the committee gaped at Ivy, her brown pinafore dress, brass buckle across tummy, red check polyester blouse, laced-up boots.

"Now," she leant forward, "in compliance with the Glebe pledge, which was, as I recall, the phrase used by Plum, I demand to know how this primitive decision was arrived at by one or more of you without my knowledge." She tapped on the table with a forefinger. "What I demand from the committee is a copy of regulation 4(c)."

Jove, mouth open, looked to the deputy chair who looked to the chair.

"One of you will have access to the regs governing eviction."

"Not here," replied Mrs. Hotch. "But in essence what 4(c) sets out is," she sucked in a breath, "that in certain circumstances eviction may be resorted to, and I'm afraid, Mrs. Gorwick, your conduct falls into that category."

"What category are we talking about?"

Dorita Gittings said, making an owl-like face, "Why don't you find out how the decision was reached?"

"Well how? If I've done nothing culpable."

Mrs. Hotch rolled her eyes. "You pushed Aggie Pont in the utility room."

"All I did was reach for the machine and the woman happened to be in the way."

"You deliberately pushed her while she was operating the clothes washer."

"That's rubbish."

"You got everyone up in the middle of the night for nothing. Mrs. Bover, close to her hundredth birthday, caught cold."

"Wurll," said Ivy, reverting to dialect, "that were unfortunate but I dint instruct her to leave the building."

"She went outside because she believed the house was burning."

"That was Clem's idea."

In the hush Dorita Gittings resumed, "You called on the housekeeper to serve you tea in bed in the middle of the night."

"That's another lie."

The Reverend Goth put an unlighted cigarette between his lips.

"You came down to lunch in improper attire," said the chair.

"You can't evict an old party for that."

"You're irascible."

"That's your version," Ivy splayed a hand on the table. "I'm an honest person. Worked hard all me life. Always told the truth. Tried to serve as best I could and now that I'm losing steam I'm faced with this. Well, let me clarify." She made a fist with her hand. "You won't get away with treating a woman of eighty-five like this. You'll see!" She eyed each member in turn, spun round and strode towards the opening door.

"It's hard to get through to these zombies," Ivy told her daughter at the foot of the stairs. "I feel like zapping the whole lot. The only language they understand is money. But I got to play me part, eh? The last thing I want to do is please the buggers but what alternative is there? If I donate to their conservatory fund, say five thousand, it'd save a lot of shouting."

Five grand here, ten grand there, Triss thought, out goes two, out goes three, out goes another one and that means me.

"What we gonna do now, Marty?" Ivy paused in swaggering back and forth across the hall.

"I don't know about you," replied Triss, "I'm taking myself out for strong coffee."

Ivy winked and raised a thumb. "You're on. Except," with a keen look, "I got to stop in to pay the papers."

24 THE GENERAL HAS A PLOY

"Hell-o there, Mrs. Gorwick," said the newsagent from behind the shoulder-high chocolate counter. "Your total comes to nine forty-three with VAT. All right are we?"

"Since you ask, I'm anything but. You heard dint you, about the bus that hurled me from one end to the other? Yeh, had to spend three days in hospital."

"Oooh my!"

"And now they're talking eviction." She turned about to face the queue of shoppers. "That's right, throwing an old woman out in the street."

"Never! You don't mean that new place up the road?"

"That's right."

"Whatever for?"

"I wasn't dressed right for lunch."

As they quit the newsagent's Ivy said, "I better get something to read."

Inside the mobile library Triss, leaning on the counter, held back an eye-roll as a similar tale unfolded and all page turning ceased. By the time they reached the Café Belge, via the optician's, the story had started to roll.

"Any joy over lunch?" Triss inquired as she spread margarine over a toasted wholemeal bun.

"Inmates keep themselves to themselves. But ever so *khaind* on the surface...Chraist Almaighty what's this? Teabag with no label? Water off the boil? In a cup? I ordered a pot. I can't drink this muck."

"Wouldn't it be better at this stage to take a few days off? Have a holiday?"

"Holiday!" Ivy yelled, removing her hearing aid. "You're the one that wants the holiday, first class on the boat and you stretched out on the deck. Well, I'm making that donation and that's all there is to it."

"Perhaps you ought to underwrite the whole glasshouse. It might buoy up the spirits. Make the 'inmates' beg you to stay. Imagine old Mother Gorwick rated Number One in the popularity poll. I can hear Dorita Gittings at the AGM! It gives me great pleasure to introduce, as our keynote speaker, Ironclad Ivy the Irate!"

"I know," Ivy pointed a finger. "You're wild because your share's going down."

"As far as my share goes, let it go down to the basement. Piss it away, piss everything away." Triss's neck started to burn. "I've had it with you, Mum. Had it." Snatching her coat and hoisting her satchel she pushed open the teashop door and headed for the bus stop.

Down the road, the Jaguar was waiting to exit the Glebe driveway. A minute later it stopped in front of the café and Plum appeared, leaving the winkers on. As he shuffled round her, talking in hushed tones, the phrase, "What you fail to recognize," pounded some inner gong.

Head lowered, Triss broke into the boardroom aura. "Ever thought to recognize a daughter with a penn'orth of insight?" Putting up one hand in a Stop signal, she snarled, "Oyez Women All! See what we've got here! None other than Jovian Plum, glorified accountant, triple A winner of some trumped up award! With a lifestyle to uphold! A cat to dump!"

"Beatrice, please! Try to see me as a sort of ally."

"Ally!" she choked. "One who's thrown my mother out in the street?!"

From the Café Belge, a green double-decker was seen nosing the curve and just as Triss decided to run for it, the teashop's curtained door burst open, with a voice cooing, "There she is! Didn't I tell you she wouldn't be a minute?"

The hunched figure, escorted out with eyes gimlet and mouth taut, broke into a big smile at Plum's approach. "All along I knew me eviction was none of your doing. And you'll be relieved to learn, sir, that I have decided to live with it." That, and Ivy's flattering reassurances that deceit was not in Plum's nature, caused Triss to shrink back under the teashop awning.

After the lingering handshake, Ivy lurched against her daughter, "I'm shrammed and I got to get back. So don't stand there like a sack of spuds. Get inside and pay the shop. I come out without me purse."

25 THE BATTLE JOINED

Knocks on her door grew urgent, making Ivy, dousing her dentures, sing out, "You'll have to wa-ait" to two young men, one with spiked red hair in skin-tight trousers and Mexican waistcoat, the other in a dark suit.

"We're Cable South Television."

Ivy clunked her teeth in place. "I say, don't shoot me yet."

The hip younger man grinned as he heaved a device off his shoulder.

"We're here to tape an interview."

"What, now?"

"Are you Mrs. Ivy Gorwick?"

"That's me all right. You must have seen the hairdresser's petition!"

"Saw your case in the *Daily Scope: Retirement Home Scandal*."

"Well, I'm blowed!"

"Are you ready?"

"You fellers don't give us a lot of notice."

"Spontaneity's what gets the ratings."

"Gawd," she muttered. "Give me a minute or two to put on a bit of rouge."

The first Wednesday in October, Triss pushed opened mother's door to a party: Clem, the WRAC and Evie, mother's patient, around a tea urn, scones, jam and cream with sorbet, and Ivy urging, "Come in or stay out." In pedal pushers and lime green baseball cap, she padded over to insert the video.

To applause, cameras zoomed into a close-up of the sleek-haired man reporting deviations in care at certain senior residences. While Clem poured tea and Evie the milk, two familiars appeared on screen and Ivy turned up the sound.

"Wurll," she boomed in the TV's frame, "I lark der place all right. Yeh always larked the Glebe Repose. I'm settled." The Ivy bed-sitting room had somehow morphed into a stage set with arc lights.

"But they're evicting you before Christmas!" declared the man with the mic. "Why would they take that step?"

"Me sight's not too grand and I can't hear as I used to."

"But you can fend for yourself." The anchorman brought the microphone near.

"Eh?"

"You don't require nursing care?"

"No, I don't. I'm ambulant. I'm continent. And more to the point I've hung onto one or two marbles." (Laughter)

"There must be more to this?"

"I got evicted by the Board for wearing slippers to tea. But what's not generally realized is I dint feel up to much that day. I tried to appill but there's no appill. They wouldn't listen to me. Me! Ivy Gorwick, treated like a mental case just because she's eighty-five years old! The point is, she can perform! Like numerous dressings on Mrs. Cash's varicose ulcer!"

The camera cut to a close-up of Evie lifting her leg, then zoomed in on the mauvish scar. "You can hardly see it now." (Applause)

Holding the sugar cone mic, the anchorman concluded, "Mrs. Gorwick never received a first warning; regulation 4(c), justifying eviction, turned out to be fictional. Despite its polished interiors and Japanese garden, the Glebe Repose is lagging behind its mandate. The question hanging in the air is: How can these heartless homes be monitored? Tune in next week to another installment in our series: 'Aging With Dignity.'"

26 TRISS AND DELIE

"I say, you do look awfully down in the mouth," Delie said, poking around in Triss's bag for the Airedale's Vege-Biccy. "One doesn't have to be a moon of Pluto. Try living each day fully."

"My days are overstuffed as it is. That bloody Zoltan went and told cook I'm not up to the job." Triss struggled to restrain the Airedale charging the mastiff. "All I did was drop spinach on a wineglass. If I'd had the moxie I'd have dumped it on him!"

They trudged on, Delie enquiring after the General.

"Got a new aspect: 'You-people-must-know-who-I-am!' I pray it won't skew her chances of staying on." Triss grabbed two collars at the park's revolving grille. "There is one pinhole of light. In dealings with authority Mum will toe the line."

"Hardly seems to have toed many lines up to now."

"Sees equals as subordinates. What's a sergeant to a general?"

Delie turned round. "Ah that Clement woman! 'D'you know? My grandfather once met Lord Dollgordon?'" All six dogs through the grille, she called over her shoulder, "How would Mama define authority?"

27 EVICTION

At two-fifteen Ivy staggered into the dining room and, dropping her hearing aid on a side plate, reached across to the remains of the shepherd's pie. Clem, Hope, Aggie, Lil, Dolly, Ida, Evie, plus a new resident, Dotsy, were in a huddle, hands jiggling and heads wagging. Ivy, scraping up the last of the Brussels sprouts, shoved her plate aside and reached over to the marmalade pudding, tuning in to Garcia reciting for Remembrance Sunday the names of related heroes including Ralph Gorwick. And adding an announcement:

Dear Residents:

Due to corporate consolidation and management change, resident conditions, all with the well-being of residents in mind, are under reconsideration. Glebe Repose requests your indulgence during this difficult period.

Jovian Plum,

Administrator

Ivy, wiping the dessert dish with her roll, looked up and, resetting her hearing aid, called out, "What's it all about?"

Hope, turning to her, mimed one word: "Mov-ing."

With all residents talking at once, nothing could be made out until certain phrases echoed and re-echoed: "Everywhere you looked…Firemen!… Who?… Her, the Gorblimey!"

Ivy leant forward, mouth full. "You bitches can't lay all this on me! What the bloody hell has it got to do with Ivy?"

Hope, directing the full force of loathing, whispered, "A question of her ways."

"Me ways are better thought out than any inmate in this room."

In the tense silence Lila whispered, "We mean conduct that doesn't measure up."

"To what? Your *ivver so naice* standards?"

"The TV show might have aggravated things," Clem Dollgordon put in with a nod, "a tiny bit much for the Glebe."

"Two blokes with telly paraphernalia show up at my door!" Ivy roared. "You," pointing to Garcia, "didn't have to bring the buggers upstairs."

"The crux is," Hope rejoined, "a motion for your eviction was carried by the Board. And by the Grace of God there's no way to reverse it."

28 GREENRAY

"Look here, Beat, you've got to get me out of here! At the double! You got no choice...To find me a place! Glebe's taken over by the bloody Stellarmount.... Old Duchesses shipping out to a Victorian pile on a back road."

"I'm pushed for time, Mum."

"Pushed for time? Pushed for money! Never made much of your life did you? Never did get any sense of direction."

The line went dead until Ivy heard a firm "Shan't come till Wednesday."

"I said today."

"Not today."

"They can't add on any conservatory now so they won't be needing my donation, will they?"

Triss's recollection of the one Home Ivy had not objected to was the one Mr. Cardross had not recommended. What were the doctor's words? Spare was it? Sparse? Or stark? The Greenray's washed exterior evoked carefree mornings on the sands at San Remo, front turf smooth as a bowling green. But flanked by a straight line of six identical trees! True, no rambler roses graced the back fence but could the curved silhouette, behind the sorrel, turn out to be a plastic flamingo?

A few minutes down the road, buttoning her coat against a chill November wind, Triss entered a hall faded to drab, with ceiling-to-floor cracks and piles of sheetrock panels. Rita the matron, a squat figure in an aqua nylon overall, led through dining and TV areas, both commodious. One point against was her lack of starch. No starched cap or cuffs! No cap or cuffs! Still, the vacant room's five walls and two windows faced a patio with cupressas. The clincher was the rent.

That afternoon, Ivy in her favourite dufflecoat, and Triss, holding the umbrella, crossed at the Belisha beacon. The front lawn got the nod. In a survey of the roost, Ivy commended the three-sided exposure and fitted cupboards, disparaging the washbasin's and WC's seniority. Triss chewed her fingers.

"Three meals served," said the matron. "Dining room. Cardroom. Sun lounge. Hip bath with hoist. Nurse on duty. Laundry. Tea and Snacks at 4 PM. Hot chocolate at nine-thirty. Press the bell for tea, coffee, biscuits, whatever else you fancy in the middle of the night."

Triss, behind mother strutting through the TV lounge, heard, "Cloud Nine."

Things moved with despatch. For a nominal fee the plasterer offered van service. He and Triss made three trips for Ivy's effects, minus what the new room could not hold, while Ivy toured bathrooms, laundry and sunroom. "I'm hanging onto the the chest of drawers," Ivy warned. "That housekeeper's not getting it."

Triss's right temple throbbed, indicating oncoming headache. "You can't hang on to every last widget!" she cried. "In a smaller space!"

"I'll have you know I'm paying more."

The plasterer turned out to be Reg the owner. His battered face, missing incisor, and his lingering gaze gave off competing signals: one moment rascal, next moment salt of the earth. Taking Ivy and Triss aside, he said, "We don't bother the residents." He continued, "We let them please theirselves. Except I have to deadbolt the street door because last Saturday night a pair of ladies went out and had one in the Red Lion. In their nightgowns! Raggedy Reg they call me. But I'm the one with a few bob in the bank and I've only just turned fifty."

Ivy looked up, "Strewth, is that all! I made sure you were more'n that. You look like Father Time!"

"While we're setting up the room perhaps you'd like to take your mother out?"

"Out of the building?"

"Anywhere."

"Mum, we're going out for arabica."

"I fill like a glass of stout."

"I am not in the mood for any smoke-filled bar."

The hour was sunny with a bite in the wind and the Café Belge was jampacked. Eventually settled at a corner table, Ivy pronged the table mat with a pastry fork, muttering, "You got plenty to answer for." Biting with difficulty into a toasted bacon sandwich, she added, "Underwear here, pyjamas where? In with photo frames and library books, you say! I can't even find one decent pair of drawers."

"I do what I can and that's all I can do."

"And stop scratching! Spare a few shekels for a medicated shampoo." Waving the sandwich, "Sprucing up in a black parka, cat hair down the front! You can't dress middle punk at your age!"

With pressure over her right eye, Triss clasped hands under the table praying to the All for an end to delays at the coffee machine.

Ivy's lower lip came forward. "You'll be surprised to know why I'm glad to get shot of the Glebe," she said and leant forward. "Last night I had a visitor."

Sipping the freshly ground, brewed blend, served at the correct point below boiling, Triss felt the world slowly gliding into sync.

"Visitor, I said. In purple robes, shot with green. Draped over the edge of my armchair."

"Evie Cash," Triss murmured.

"Nothing like her."

Triss clasped the oversized cup in both hands. "Maybe Aggie?"

"I said, visitor wearing a hood. Are you taking this in?"

"Did it carry a scythe?"

"A what?"

"Was it all in black?"

"I said purple shot with green for Chrissake!"

"You mean you saw a ghost?"

"I don't know about that but I will say this, it seemed sort of considerate."

Triss, basking in caffeine-induced relief, whispered, "The sun will play tricks with shadows. On a day like this, how would you like to go out for a stroll?"

"You know I can't stroll and even if I could stroll, where would I stroll to?"

"We could get a ride out the front."

"I told you what the inmates said about the Pier and I am not spending the whole afternoon clocking up a taxi!"

29 SHADOW

The following Wednesday the 9.40 Pompey from Waterloo came to more than one dead stop between Rowlands Castle and Havant. Triss, in reverie, was age eight in North End, leaving the milk van clutching a half pint, and a shilling short in the change, father aiming a scrubbing brush at her head! Tears and more tears building up to memories of earlier tears and Mum's defence of Dad's resentment. And now a phantom dispatch: "All those tears! What for? There's no need to cry. All you have to do is tune Dad out!"

The Greenray's front door opened onto ladders, planks, paint pots and no decorators. The time was 12.15. At the front window mother swung round, "Oh hullo!" Her room, set up with divan along eye-level window, clothing and doodads out of sight, green paper chains hung with tinsel and a single red balloon. Dropping her duffle coat, Triss remarked that with all the painting and plastering, they had somehow managed to jolly the place up.

"Christmas just a week away for Chrissake!" Ivy cried. "I don't suppose you ever bother with a tree."

"Never a dead tree," replied Triss with pride. "Look, Mum, the Coach and Horses puts on a Christmas buffet from twelve to three: hors d'oeuvres to kumquats. I can order a taxi now. Table booked in October."

Mother sighed, "Well…" then shook her head. "Can't. My belly's all at sea." Mumbling about distension and dyspepsia, she shuffled to the bay window, halted, half turned and froze.

"You might manage one or two of the smaller courses."

Jaw clenched, Ivy looked round, then, with eyes half closed, gave a parade ground bellow: "Ivy Gorwick's life has been…Third Rate!" The room knitted up in tension. "If I'd had the gumption to enter the nursing corps at the outbreak, I could've had a life. Been made Major easy! Might have got to half Colonel! But, lucky old Ivy, along comes Sapper

Gorwick, orphaned at four, rest of family gone. Three times I give the bloke back his ring. He threatened suicide!" She trod the room, three steps up, two back, "Me of all people stuck with him, house and kid!" She swung round. "I could have been first in line for Matron, no sweat. With me perfection in sutures and me top colonics!" She lowered an index finger, "Night staff sneaking pills off the dispensary shelf and guess who was on the carpet?" She sighed. "Wurl, these days the post of Matron's gone for a Burton. Now it's all computers and girls in mini-suits marching about with files."

Triss collected mysteries and thrillers and piled them near the door. Ivy, fiddling with magnifying glass and reading lamp, gathered up the *Daily Scope.* Then letting it fall, roared, "Victimized from Day One! Passed the 11-plus and barred from the Sec to take charge of kid brother! At fourteen walking the streets!" She made a chewing motion, "And, sixty-odd years later, what do I wind up as? A bloody linen cupboard Super! And while we're on the subject, Beat, I might as well tell you I've got to get out of this place."

"Please!"

"Here's me in Half-Wit House. Married couple watching TV with the sound turned off. I ask the woman the time. Looked at me, blank like! There's five shaky dads playing cards all day long. Any amount of old grans staggering round. None of 'em's even up to saying Howdy!"

Triss flattened herself against the wall.

"I'll tell you what else," Ivy yelled. "The shadow's here. On me chair." Groaning, she reached for the remote, dropped it and, shaking the zip on her pinafore dress, barked orders, "Find me pyjamas! Turn the set round. I'm watching 'Barricades' in bed!"

Triss patted the armchair. "It's not even noon."

"I fill like dozing off."

"Should I try for the 1.14?"

Ivy removed one shoe and flung it on the floor, shouting, "Get me my pills!"

Triss put a glass of water on the bedside table and counted pills out of a vial.

"Get Cardross!"

"Why? If you're not sick."

"What do you know?"

"How are you feeling?"

Ivy lay back whispering, "As if I don't belong to myself."

"I can't tell him that."

"Get him."

Triss lifted the telephone. "Mum's insistent...Emergency!.. The Greenray.... He'll be over in two shakes."

"I know him and his two shakes," rubbing her nose, and screaming, "I got to void."

Triss dragged over the commode. As mother didn't co-operate she tried lifting. "When I slide the pot under, be prepared to raise yourself. Now, LIFT!"

"I'm losing it," Ivy muttered.

Soon Triss was being aided by two cheery women. "Come on my lovely, can you move this leg for me?"

Within twenty minutes an enigmatic Cardross strode in. "When is the last time you had a poop?" he said, twinkling at Triss.

"Tell him to stop mucking about."

"I think you might go in for a check." The doctor wrapped up the stethoscope and scribbled notes on a pad. "Don't worry, we'll find you a bed. Now Ms. Beatrice, I'll ask you to hand this note to the physician in charge. You'll recognize the ward, Ivy. Today it's called Acute Female."

For what seemed like hours, daughter sat in silence, mother groaning "Where's the bloody ambulance?"

As Triss dunked a Garibaldi biscuit into a mug of instant coffee, two men in gray and white uniforms entered, and enclosed Ivy in a red blanket. Cursing the frost, she was carried five steps down to the oval driveway, lowered onto a stretcher and slotted into the ambulance. Driver and stretcher-bearer worked as one. Triss's experience with injured cats had cautioned against expectations, making her unprepared for the consideration shown her mother as not the fourteenth casualty of the day, but the only one. Heartless may be cool these days, Triss thought, studying the wart on the driver's hairy neck, but look at the way they're handling her gripes!

Along the QA hospital corridors they trundled, passing an Honours List, including Ivy's name, to a long ward with a lifelike Christmas tree. Once settled in bed four left, Ivy stopped groaning, and muttered to Triss kneeling on the floor, "You never warned me about leaving my home. Never bothered to tell me what I was getting into."

"I tried," Triss whispered.

"From your side of the fence, not out of caring for me. You never have listened. Never learned from me. And I'm warning you now. Cats won't get you anywhere!"

Two doctors at the end of the bed, one in a black pinstriped suit, the other in grey miniskirt and black cardigan, conferred on heart scan, rectal exam, sedation, drip feed. Catheter.

Triss put both elbows on the bedcover and whispered into mother's ear, "I never can forget the poor brown tabby at Number 56 Battenberg."

A staff nurse pointed Triss to the Relatives Room where, next to the coffee urn, she unzipped a boot to massage a big toe joint. Soon a youngish man wearing a nametag that identified him as the Senior Registrar briskly made straight for her, with news that due to an abdominal event, the occupant of bed number four had been wheeled to X-ray.

"We don't know the origin. In fact," the Senior Registrar added with a sad smile, "there's a lot our profession doesn't know."

"Is she in pain?"

"She's had to be sedated."

Triss thought for a moment then whispered, "Should we wait?"

"They can't be taking me down," Ivy muttered. "How can I be dead if I'm here?" Wheeled along chilly corridors, overtaken by a blood-splattered stretcher case, staff nurse and two orderlies, "Me of all babes winding up in Gunner Street! With the riffraff!"

Lifted onto the table, she put out a hand to clutch at the green-clad doctor standing over her. Images swirling around, she muttered, "Once I had status." Echoes resounded across the years, orders in the blanket telling her to find a way! I'll try sleep, she decided. The docs are all actors. Make a big thing out of consulting relatives. Wind up playing it their way.

The x-ray room recast in shades of mauve, awash in faint light and lavender mist hanging over the stretcher, in and out of shadows' imperatives: *Lose no time. Dally is delay.* She saw what appeared to be a pile of stage props, manifesting as a forlorn party of females, some kneeling, a few crouching, one out flat. She tried prayer until out of the turbulence a blue light arose, winking, coming close, fading, reappearing at the limits of sight. Moments later, it opened out to reveal billowing interiors. Dissolved in blueness she watched a tiny monitor lead through a telescope to figures lifting her head. Conflict returned, an urge to move, the need to stay. Voices: "We could get a priest if you like." Triss's shrill, "She used to charge up and down this ward in her dusky blue dress, navy belt and silver buckle." Inside the curtain, where her giant-sized daughter sat, Ivy noted black globs on the eyelids.

The cot had returned to its place. In the visitors' room a junior nurse summoned Triss. "Within the hour she'll regain consciousness," she said, indicating a pink stick to moisten Ivy's mouth. "The canteen's near closing time. Better go and get yourself a bite."

Triss couldn't shake visions of Ivy's wartime service: pips for the nine o'clock news, signal to slam on a peaked cap, grab her gray raincoat with the red chevrons, mount the no-speed bike without checking the tyres, pedal six miles under tracer bullets, flares and occasional falling shrapnel. "You must have made quite a few of our boys comfortable in them days," the grocer had once remarked.

Giving up on the canteen, oblivious to time, Triss crept back. A night nurse came out of the gloom to guide her to a side ward.

At 6 AM mother was fast asleep and daughter checking health magazines for dairy-free recipes. A trolley halted at the end of the bed with two teas, sugarless and milked, and two finger mince tarts. Setting one mug on the bedside table, Triss sat sipping and called out, "Tea's here!" Ivy grunted and did an elbow stretch. Triss, leaning over, heard, "Cats don't pay the rent," as a shaky hand slid the mug over and drained it without spilling a drop.

"I do try to be a better daughter," Triss began.

"Yeh?" Ivy groaned, leaning into the bank of pillows. "I'm buggered if you do." Her breath had a rasp to it.

An Asian nurse, in a brown striped dress, came to sit on the other side of Ivy. She took the pink stick from Triss and inserted a fresh one. After a while she got up and stood with her head on one side. Then pulled the curtains round.

"Hold her hand," the nurse commanded, holding Ivy's other hand. The rasping grew softer. Triss took up the pink stick and continued moistening her mother's mouth.

Ivy, on her back, lay perfectly still. An air of triumph had come over her. Pale green arose as in a vessel moving up her bare arms transforming her chest and neck, flooding them and the pink face in greenish milky white.

30 VIGIL'S END

Triss had witnessed the last heartbeat, yet did not accept it. She turned to the young nurse who, nodding sadly, took her hands. Triss broke down. It seemed the thing to do. Theatre.

Back in the side ward with hot tea she sat through an influx of emotion, fear yielding to chaos. Then a new undercurrent threaded its way to the surface. My, that was soon over! Quick and painless. But wait, are they sure?

A first-year nurse with rolled-up sleeves and elasticated cuffs stood by, "The first thing we'd better do is telephone the family. While she's still in the ward. I believe she has a brother?"

Triss blew her nose, "How would you know?"

"Listed as Next of Kin."

"Died!" Art whistled, "How can she have died when she'd only just got settled?...View her! No, I can't come. I'd rather remember her... No. Not coming...I told you. I don't want to."

The young nurse led Triss back to the curtained cubicle. Pillows had been removed and Ivy lay straightened out with large nostrils pointing up. Triss stared at her alabaster mother a long time. Ivy wore an expression of considerable dignity. Dignity in death seemed, of all things, comical. The body resembled a wax prototype of some world-famous comedian. Charlie Chaplin. Groucho Marx. Hilarity stirred somewhere deep in Triss's gut, rising to the chest area, welling around, vibrating arms and shoulders until silent laughter engulfed her. Never in her life had she shaken from head to foot. There was nothing for it but to stand there letting the strain confine the stomach muscles. Swaying to and fro, she held her sides. Strange concepts came in: None of this is serious. All Pretend. Shaking all over, she lowered herself into the visitor's chair and leaned over the body, trying to close out alien thoughts. But like vapour they sat, lending lightness to her mood, assuring her that ruts and obstacles would iron out.

A vision of smooth sailing moved in. Before long you'll be home and dry. Forget anxiety about renewing the lease or paying the vet. An end to waitressing at that god-forsaken bistro. Recycling depot duty down to two days a week. Relief dogwalking only. She let go of mother's freckled hand, still warm, and peeped between the bed curtains. The rest of the ward had woken up to clatter of spoons and rustle of Christmas wrap. Slowly she backed out, meeting the Senior Registrar's handclasp and rueful comment on Nature's mediation. At the main desk, a sleepy receptionist handed her a brochure on how to secure the Death Certificate.

31 CHRISTMAS

Seven-thirty on Christmas morning and time had stopped. Mists softened the harbour lights as Triss navigated the car park and picked her way down the stepped path. Turning left at the bottom she came to a frosted window with plastic mini-spruces. A neon sign flickered: *Hot Coffee Open*. After rattling the door, she continued downhill. At the bus stop, she hoisted her satchel and took off. Under the dark blanket of sky, waves of content started to flow. On the Truck Stop Café door there was a notice in faded scribble: Hot Porridge. She wrenched open the storm door, believing that at long last the holidays had begun.

At nine-thirty in the Greenray's festooned and deserted dining room, Triss, over reheated coffee, regaled the mournful Reg with her version of formalities surrounding a death: funeral expenses and compassionate leave.

"The Home would like as many of her clothes as you can spare because these old souls don't seem to have a rag to call their own," Reg commented, his imponderable eyes resting on her. "What I mean is, after the family have been, we'll clear out the rest for you at no extra charge. The rent's paid till the end of the month so if you can't get home and back you might want to doss down here."

At the ground floor corridor, Triss stopped dead. Outside her mother's room was a tartan shopping cart. An ancient man, in a suit several sizes too large, squeezed past. Someone was peering through gaps in a door ajar. Triss crept up to mother's door, hesitated, then threw it open, making Art simultaneously spring off the bed and thrust the file he was holding down between mattress and bedhead.

"Beaty, my lover," he began, "we're in shock. All of us. One moment she's her own cranky self, next moment..."

"I didn't expect to see *you* here!" Her tone rose up in mid-sentence. "I mean, what the hell are you doing here at this time of the morning? And on Christmas!"

"Well, lover, I didn't expect to see *you* today."

"You haven't answered my question."

"Only looking over stuff."

Triss bent over. "What are Mum's papers doing under the bed?"

Art pointed to the accordion file, "I lent it to her. Now I need it."

"I'd have been glad to empty it out for you to collect."

"But lover, how am I supposed to know you'd still be around?"

A haggard Triss put two hands to her head crying, "I've come from the bedside!"

He stood there unhurried and well-disposed, forcing her to revert to gentle enquiry, "Was there something particular you need...?"

"One of her bills came to me and I wanted to check it had been paid."

"Which bill was that?"

"Prescription sunglasses."

"May I see the bill?"

"I didn't bring it with me."

Triss gritted her teeth. "Leave it for now, Art. I'll pop into the opticians. When I get a chance."

She lifted the accordion file, checked inside, and handed it to Art, urging him to the door. Tailing him through the TV room, past the waxwork couple, she cried out, "Why would she ask *you* to pay bills?"

"When you weren't available, like."

"I always am available."

At the front gates, Triss wedged a foot against the cart's front wheel and blurted out, "Is it really a bill you're after? Or might it be something else? Like the Will?"

"Will!" Art replied in a conversational tone. "Why would I want to search out the Will when it's held by the solicitor? Personally I don't care too much about it." His expression was relaxed, one eye half closed. "Even so," he added in his languid way, "As her brother I've got just as much right to see the Will as you have. In any case she's given me Power of Attorney."

Triss began to tremble, "With me the official Next of Kin?"

"Not only because I'm a blood relation but because I'm competent."

One foot in the gutter, legal terms rattling round in her head, Triss held down the screaming inside, saying in a hushed tone, "You may not know that your sister's Will incorporates my father's estate. Are you convinced of your right to dispense his life savings?"

"I'll do my best to administer the Will according to my sister's wishes."

The traffic light flashed green and two gigantic tour buses rumbled along the London Road.

"Answer me this," Triss shouted. "Wouldn't you rather turn the whole thing over to me?"

"Well, I wouldn't," he whispered into her ear, "because she was definite in her need of my involvement."

"My mother," Triss panted, "not cold, and the putative next of kin sneaks in to scrabble around for the Will."

"Beaty, you're getting all aerated! As a blood relation, though, I got every right to see it. Ask the solicitor."

Teeth chattering, she stammered, "You've been hanging around ever since she sold the house."

"No, you're the one hanging around. I'm on the spot."

With a spurt she rushed at the shopping cart and overturned it. A sad sack, it lay on the verge, one wheel spinning. She ran back to her mother's room, checked for Will through papers on floor, bed and in kitchen cupboard. Fifteen minutes later she saw Art outside the bay window, swinging the shopping cart back and forth like a mower. "Any luck?" he called out.

Hand on heart, she took her time walking round to the patio. "You will tell me what you've done with the Will," she said in measured tones, "or I'll call the police."

Art turned out all pockets: ballpoint pens, sweet wrappers, smudged shop receipts, grocery stamps, over the crazy paving. Unzipped the shopping bag and turned it inside out. They stared each other down, until Art cocked his head, "All of us are in shock."

"A pack of hyenas," she panted, "no, worse. Humans! With your cut flowers and your hundred teabags. Sending grown kids sniffing round auntie with cards in code to read, "Any spare cash? Forget me not!""

Art closed his small mouth, bent down to pick up the mess, quietly zipped the bag and wheeling the cart away, turned with a nod and "Happy Christmas!"

Praying for total absorption in the All, Triss eventually touched on a zone of calm enabling her to find a payphone, leave messages for Delie, bistro and recycling depot. She turned mother's mattress, remade the bed and, in a pair of her pyjamas, collapsed in it. The Greenray was as silent as a locked church. Even the waxwork couple had vanished.

Next morning she set out for the offices of Crate & Crate, Solicitors. Passing the Co-op, open and deserted, fish-and-chip shop padlocked, she espied sign-writing in an upper window and entered the solicitors' street doorway. Halfway up the stairs she met a haggard woman coming down who said, "Closed till next week featuring the Free Style and Blow-Dry starting Monday….Crate the solicitor! Packed up weeks ago! I must get that sign taken down. Left no number. Moved to Tangier."

Passing the Chinese take-away, Triss turned back and, without mentioning MSG or free range, ordered Egg Foo Yung to stay. The owner brought a glass of jasmine tea and aspirins, wishing her happy holidays. At the Greenray she found Reg watching football reruns in the deserted lounge and learned that Art had laid claim to Ivy's TV, hifi, radio and jewellery.

Holding a hot compress to her head, Triss looked up Crate in the phone book and dialed. "Hilary Crate speaking. No, Jared, my brother, resigned. Thing is the firm went bust which exacerbated his midlife crisis. Had to take himself off somewhere warm. Office files? I'd have to ring you back. A Will? Ah. Try the Central Deaths Registry."

32 FUNERAL

In addition to family, eleven other mourners, all carless, showed up at the Last Post Funeral Parlour. Art, puffy round the eyes, took it upon himself to select who in the party should ride with whom. The extended confab and last minute switching made it hard for Triss to focus on the undertaker's directions for completing the grant application. He finally surrendered a tiny plastic box. Inside was Ivy's wedding ring on a cube of foam rubber.

The funeral procession made its way along the saltmarsh of Triss's childhood. Wedged between Dolly and daughter Juliane, she sat forward to avoid Dolly's picture hat. A fine rain, untrue to forecast, had settled into a cat-and-dog pelt bringing deathbed scenes to light: Omar's black teeth, Maw's mildewed petticoat.

The cortège ascended a humped railway bridge, deflecting Triss to memories of a late night loiter with a youth met on the last bus, protracted talk of penis calibre, stopping not far short of consummation, the site remaining a fantasy for forbidden erotica, specifically down the green bank behind the brambles.

Dolly snuggled up to Triss, "He's been having nightmares."

Triss, clearing her throat, looked daggers at Art's silhouette.

"Wakes me up in the middle of the night." Dolly clasped Triss's arm, "Claims there's a monk at the end of the bed!"

Triss whispered, "Were its robes purple shot with green?"

Dolly tapped on the glass partition. "Arty. Was the monk in purple and green?...Couldn't look, he says. I had to give him two hot water bottles, one for his stomach, one under his knees." Dolly steered her hat. "His wrists were like ice."

Inside the chapel Art, at the altar, arms spread out in the manner of host, shuttled the newsagent, hairdresser, librarian, Evie Cash, Garcia and Plum to pews, signalling seated mourners to move over.

Triss had been put out by the undertaker's manner and the price of the casket, remaining convinced that no hardwood coffin with brass handles ever got cremated. The fact that all that was left of a mother was inside a box on the altar was bad enough. But what if Ivy had already been incinerated and her ashes consigned to a wrong niche in the garden of rest, making the service in honour of someone else's mother? Or father! Unable to tune in to the priest's invocation, she sat face in hands until Art kneed her, murmuring, "All over, lover." Looking up to burgundy dralon curtains closing out the coffin, she put an arm out to hold Art back and seized the curate's hand.

"Your mother would have been pleased to know of the number who came to pay their respects," the young cleric said with a puckish smile.

"I took it on myself," she sniffed, "to add 'No Flowers' to the obit notice." The curate took her elbow and led her out to the pergola.

"Mr. Cardross will see him," Dolly pressed Triss's other arm, "so we mustn't overstay at the pub. Though hot toddy and a warm pastie might pull him round."

Plum, in the funeral line, threw Triss an obscure look as she swept by. At the barred doorway the next funeral party was overflowing into the chapel. Leaving the pergola, the curate and Triss set off in the direction of memorial plots but were forced back by the wind. Raincoats flapped as mourners had to turn and go, via the side gate, to the car park where a single eddy lifted a plastic bag, spiralled it round and thrust it smack into Art's face, making him skid and land in the mud. No one in the funeral party noticed except Dolly, who hurried back, and Triss, who saw it as an omen. The ruffled limousine driver packed the front seat with newspaper.

Parking space behind Martha Brickwoods was eventually located after two tours of the nearby roundabout. Once inside, the old lounge reminiscent of Omar, the party relaxed enough to dry out, warm up, and turn with relief to the bar: spirits, wines, ales, juice, coffee, tea, chips, nuts, cheese pasties, nachos and watercress. Art, holding a balloon glass for refill, went into details of his father's defense of the Eastney Barracks cribbage title while Triss, on a barstool next to the till, shuffled and impaled drink chits. A looming Plum coming by for handshake, murmured, "Please, Beatrice, you must know,"

he hiccupped, "your mother's Notice to Quit did not, repeat not, originate with me! Nor did I support it." He stared at his hands. "Although the official signature had to be mine. But when the issue came to a vote I got the nod to abstain!"

Triss did not look up.

"If you ever need me..." Plum hurried off without even a sip of soda water.

33 SEEKING MOTHER

Under a counterpane of cats, Triss sat up in bed, rechecking for ear mites. Confiding purrs eventually brought on languor as Piper, the Colonel and Emcee moved up and vied for places. With heaviness in hollows around neck and shoulders she called out, "O Mum! Mum! Where are you?"

Over days of weary reflexes: forgetting to drop lead when the mastiff barged an approaching Rottweiler; serving pickled herring to a vegetarian; reciting flans and puddings from last week's menu, her consolation lay among the furry bodies of the night. One evening, scrubbing cat pans, she came near to calling in sick for the whole weekend.

As Triss rode to work, a mother look-alike boarded the bus: white curls close to the head, bushy frown. Triss looked away and made a mental image of features: remote gaze; powdered conk; tight pencilled lips; buff raincoat with shoes to match.

Back at work--fitting the bottle-smashing mask, rubber suit, gloves and high boots, starting the motor--disturbances came in. A mother's death takes with it a way of life. Overnight a whole era turns into history. *I must be having what Dad would have called a nervous breakup.*

After sweeping up and locking the depot, she exited a side door into the Edgware Road. That morning she had noticed a white cat in a gap between two buildings and told herself it belonged to Pizza Tops. But there it was again in the same spot, too weak to run away. Triss hurried past to the Underground, but at the ticket machine a frightful imperative descended. Spitting oaths, she returned to the alley and, crouching down, gently scooped up the bag of bones and settled it into her satchel.

The whole world had gone lame, her street paved with broken slabs, tree pits littered with cigarette ends, grocer's display of contrived junk food. The flat, squalid and cluttered, settled into familiar disorder as she bottle-fed the street cat.

Refilling twenty-one dishes, Triss announced to the waiting felines,

"The bald truth is I never can feel as I used to feel," pause in winding the tin-opener. "Seeing her death as a godsend has ruptured my sense of self. Ergo, the Will's non-appearance must be my Way Out to freedom. Mum may have had plans for me to join the human family but *my* path is along the sidelines. The threadbare life may fall below what passes for normal these days. Even so," she panted, "it's a bloody long way up from bedrock." She set cat dishes in three half circles next to the walls. "Mum never saw cat rescue, recycling, dog walks and waitressing, as alternatives to heading a human family." To the gorging household, she proclaimed, "I shall have to relinquish the Will!"

After supper Triss sat for meditation. During a half hour of otherworldly comfort, sleep intervened. Somewhere in the night a scene arose of mother in a corridor lashing out at a shadowy figure that, shaking its cloak, sent out a shower of green sparks with a proclamation, "No curtain calls for Generalissimo!"

The next morning, bed pitching, Triss awoke all at sea.

Close to their supermarket's meat department, Triss and Delie standing at a side table, handed out Nut Roast Balls on toothpicks, two-line recipes attached.

"My mama left this life," Delie whispered, "at three minutes to four PM. On the hour my sister had a visitation. A moment clear as day. Camy sensed her all around. Your mother, has she...?"

"Not a dicky bird," Triss sighed.

At five in the afternoon, Triss closed her ears to a fire engine's hee-haw on the main road and made her way down an alley whose hornbeam hedge once confined the Pin Oak Manor. Deep in memories of early days, only four cottages in the Pin Oak meadow, Triss was catapulted into the street of Now by an exotic at the party fence. Muttering, "My mother lived here," Triss watched the figure beckon, click open the gate and say, "Hang about."

A morose Triss trailed to front door and stairs to Ivy's former bedroom where, moving hanks of wool, she settled herself on a concave stool and, head in hands, tried to get a sense of Mum until a chink of bangles hinted exit. Downstairs in the old living room with the new carpet, Mrs. Singh sat her in a wicker chair. Examining Triss's hand, she whispered, "You're compatible with animals?"

Triss, managing a bleak smile, tried to dismiss the palmist's breathtaking looks, and that her own numerous two-line convergences were beyond recall. Accepting available aid, she was drawn into a warm clasp as, arm in arm, the pair swayed down the path. As the gate clicked shut, Triss stopped and looked back in confusion.

"Try to sort out where mother was happy," Mrs. Singh called. "The sunset has usually worked well for me."

Number 3 Pin Oak Lane had never looked that good, felt that good, or even smelled that good, Triss allowed, plodding up the alley, noting how regrowth of forgotten grasses lent the place a bit of style.

As a distant bell struck eight, Triss, at the Truck Stop Café, struggled into polar coat, paid the cook, and wandered into Cosham. Turning up the hill, she followed the stepped path to the hospital, joining visitors meandering along corridor after corridor. At Ivy's ward, bed four left, she stopped. The bony occupant's eyes were out on stalks.

"You all right, duckie?" came a cracked voice from the bed.

A figure pausing at the end of the bed turned to Triss. "Looking for what? Mrs. Gorwick! The wartime sister who died a fortnight ago? Your mother?" Rocking her head, the staff nurse nodded to a heavyset orderly who grasped Triss by the elbow, piloted her via the emergency lift to the basement and, keeping a tight grip, unbolted an alarm box and let her out of the building.

In an unlit corner of the grounds Triss climbed flagged steps to a stand of birches visible under the moon. Chilled to the bone, sphincteral muscles playing up, she made her way to Outpatients and, shunning the receptionist's eye, took a back seat amid wailing infants and haggard parents, and incoming road casualties.

By 10.35, numbers down to seven, she put on her coat, turned up her collar, and crept out to the January night along ghostly paths, uphill to the boundary, downhill to the main entrance. Jogging past hospital windows she tuned into manifold silences: the aged; the collision case; asthmatic toddler; lab animals. At the fourteenth lap, pooped out and glowing, she opened her coat and stretched out on a bench, gazing at a black cloud against a luminous sky. She soon started to snore.

Me happy in the grounds? Wurll, only up to a point. Hospital life can be pretty grim. Some of me glad days were up at the Hilsea Lido kids' pool when you were little. Oh yeah, your puberty caught me unawares. Sat down that Christmas night and wrote to the youth club. You were in ankle socks!

Mum in red and black, chestnut hair shingled, one foot wedged against the lamppost. Angular. Leggy. "*Where you are I'm not. The night I come out for a breather was the night of the fire.*" One arm outstretched, the flapper spun round the lamppost, black skirt soaring to reveal pale stockings and mauve garters. *"Now pay attention! The word is: Dumpty. Have you got that? Fawn dumpty. Open it up!"*

"Fiancé? Thirty-nine-year-old Iti stud drops dead! Never added up. Now all me girl's left with is cats!"

Much later, daughter shivering, pressing pain spots, jumps off the bench and limps over to the lamppost. Fumbling in pockets, out comes a chenille beret. Funny! Turns it over and pulls it down over head and ears.

"Bus you say! What now? There won't be no bus round here this side of seven in the morning. You're a bit on the early side, m'love," said the night porter. Shifting his cap to scratch, he added, "You look half-starved! Get yourself a hot drink! There's change in that machine! Call a taxi. Or wait in the warm. There's no charge."

34 A BEIGE POUFFE

Sitting up in bed, Triss stretched over to the telephone, disarranging Emcee, Geyser and Catalonia. "Then there's Art! My first sighting, him showing up for tea, uninvited! Dad out the back door like lightning! When at last Art left, out came an Xmas bundle. In October! Some piece of crap for Mum and nix for me. Only years later do I query motive. Displacement! How's that for Art expo?"

"Any more on the Will?" Delie asked.

"Central Deaths Registry says No Entry." Massaging the Colonel's ear between thumb and forefinger made his purr resound across the wires. "There's one other thing."

"What's that?"

"My Peace of Mind."

"Your what?"

"I'm awake all hours. Hot one minute. Chilled the next. Dreams that don't manifest. Were it not for my cats I'd jump out the window."

Later, as Triss was scouring cat pans with white vinegar and trilling "Jubal's Lyre," an envelope flopped on the hall mat.

The sum total of twenty-one cats, the letter ran, *brought to light by the company inspectorate, is found to be in contravention of the lease. After due consideration, the board has determined that regretfully your lease cannot be renewed.*

Face twitching, Triss went down to the main hall. Sifting through nuisance mail, she found a final electric notice and statement of vet fees for three rescues, plus the first installment of funeral expenses, a total far in excess of a month's income. For nearly an hour, twirling the beige beret, she sat musing on Mum's name for it: not buff beret, nor café au-lait beret. More like fawn. As in dumpty! A piece clunked into place.

Blanking out tinnitus, Triss eventually obeyed an urge to dial Enquiries. In some excitement, she called Garcia.

"I wondered...if, by chance, you might remember where...you think Ivy Gorwick's surplus furniture finished up?"

"I did see my relief load the settee!"

"Oh Garcia, to your knowledge were there a pair of pouffes?"

"Evie Cash took the black one."

"Did you happen to come across the...beige one?"

"There's an entry somewhere: Chattels and their Disposition. I'll look it up."

After a long wait she heard, "Arthur Parfitt: One TV, one HiFi, one taupe-colored pouffe."

At 2:00 AM Art awoke to pressure on the bedclothes and a shadow leaning over. Too nervous to yell, he lay gasping, then shuddered, prompting Dolly to swing her leg back. Pinned down, twisting the sheets, a new adage surfaced: *Avoid any central position*, which, along with Dolly's kick, brought him back from where he was.

Next morning, bemoaning new pains in the lower back, he whimpered, "Here it comes! Straight after the pill! Doll, phone the doctor's surgery!"

Dolly shrugged, "Already left two messages."

Art stiffened, "There's something on my mind. No, lis-ten," pressing head and shoulders into upholstery, "I may not make it," rubbing an eye with his fist. "So I should tell you...our Ive forgot to tell me where she kept her papers. So the day she died, it being Christmas and all, I'd thought I'd pop over to the Glebe and check on the Will. I knew the place'd be like a morgue."

"Will you answer me one thing? ONETHING? What is it in you that makes you think you can meddle? Eh?"

"I'm going to give it to you straight, lover. Cross your heart you won't tell a soul." Wincing, he propped himself up, "I'm wet through. Get a towel."

"Spit it out."

"Just as I get the Will out, the door opens and in walks Beat."

"Spare me the details."

The first Wednesday of the new year, Triss was seen dragging down the lane to Art's place. Outside, she cowered under the overhang till Dolly, spotting her from the kitchen, opened the front door, venting a strong whiff of liniment.

Putting on a half smile, Dolly whispered, "He's been ever so bad. Maybe you can jolly him up."

Rearranging himself against particle board, Art adjusted his neck pillow, "Coming through it all, are we? Anything come to light in her papers? Because to save time we oughter put in a fresh application for Probate. We got no alternative," he added with a lopsided smile.

With Art groaning, Triss, from the club chair, made a covert survey of the room. "I suppose Doll never told you that two nights running I saw a figure bending over me in bed!"

Triss's eyes paused as he folded the *Daily Scope,* telling her to ask Doll what's holding up the tea.

Dazed, Triss got up and, after scouting out the hall and front room, took the tea-tray from Dolly. In the dining room, stepping over a stack of *Daily Scopes,* she found herself looking at brown cross-stitching and French knots.

The fawn dumpty! A familiar household object, kicked around, sat on and never regarded. Eyes on Art, she set the tea tray on the low table. Even if she kissed his ring what were the chances of taking it home? When he moves I'll scoop it up and make a dash for it, she decided, milking three cups and pouring out two. But, as Mum said, he sits and sits and sits and sits.

Warming her hands on the mug, giving thanks to planters, gatherers, shippers, retailers and, with a sigh, the dairy cow, she leant forward murmuring, "Did you ever see your sister in a red and black outfit?"

Chewing on a toasted bun and fiddling with the remote, Art peered over his glasses. Eventually he replied, "Coo, it's going back a bit!" He'd begun a lengthy tea-stirring after the style of Omar. "She 'ad a favourite dress. Wore it all the time. Red top, black buttons and a black skirt."

Triss sat bolt upright, "Did you say red and black?"

"Yeh, I can see it now."

"Going back? How far back? When she was forty-five?"

"Ooh," Art wrinkled his cheek and scratched it, "Before tha-a-at. It was one of them low-waisted jobs she got 'round the time she had her hair cut off. Wurll, I was a nipper at the time so she couldn't have been much more'n twenty if that." Art pulled his personalized mug from the tray, eyes narrowing, mouth drawn tight. "She kept it for ages and I can even see her feeding Lester in that dress."

"Lester?"

"Her blackbird. Sat on her shoulder. Moved with her up to North End. Got killed by a cat."

Eyes on Art, Triss, curving her foot around the pouffe, pulled it nearer, reversed it and reached inside. Her hand met with crumpled newspaper and, under knitting patterns, a long legal envelope. Between her knees she could read in gothic script T E S T A M.... Quickly she shoved the envelope back and righted the pouffe. Hunched on the club chair, grappling with images of twenty-year-old Mum in a dress she'd never seen, she felt the room start to list.

Wiping her hands, Dolly sighed, "I'll get her a drop of brandy."

As Art picked up his remote and started flipping stations, Dolly clattered out and reappeared with a quarter bottle, pouring it into a mug. But Triss could not hold it. With hand to cheek, the mug tipped and spilled over the chair.

Dolly ran out for tissues with Art shouting, "What the bloody hell's going on?"

Triss, heaving, pulled on her jacket, staggered through the hall to the street. She left the front door open.

The sight of Triss spreadeagled on the Post Office wall might have suggested mod negative *intaglio* until, with hail coming on and no bus in sight she made a rush for the glassed-in shelter. At the South Parade terminus, she jogged along the prom, unclear about where she was until the Canoe Lake came into view. Beyond a certain coppiced birch tree, she spotted the Plum residence, where she saw Jove dithering on the front door steps, turn and put down a bag of recyclables and go inside....She followed him through the open door, across a square hall to the staircase, where a pair of removal men were tussling with a roped armoire.

A large woman in a running suit stumped down the stairs and with shy smile, held out a hand. Social obligation was in short order but Triss managed to nod as Mandy Plum marched out the front door.

"I'm making coffee for the movers," Jove puffed, stooping to retie his boot. In matted sweater, hair tangled, shiny spot revealed, he seemed not himself, scratching his sides, launching into rewards of sleeping late and no business suit. Setting down four mugs, he added, "Once resettled I intend to relieve you of Rory. In fact, Beatrice, you mightn't believe this, but Prue Bover's solicitor confirmed a codicil for care and feeding of one cat!"

In the absence of response he waited out a long pause, then straightened up, uttering the word, "Cats." Then after a pause, "Cats, Beatrice!" with an intense look.

They sat staring at the floor until Plum enquired why she had come by.

A shaking Triss belted out, "The Will!" The sound travelled hollow spaces and a removal man appeared at the door. "I saw it! At Uncle Art's inside my mother's pouffe!"

Plum spoke as to a frail elder. "Better get yourself over to Arthur's and extract that Will from the pouffe. Can you manage it?...You can't?" He added a spot of hot milk to her coffee and handed her the dish towel, "Very well then, I'll see if I can come with you."

Mopping her face she sighed, "At Mum's funeral all I fantasized were my own chances. All my life Dad refused to shell out one penny for me, what he called drag expenses, so she provided for me out of her own wages! One night coming out of the Carlton cinema I caught sight of how shrunken she looked! Deathly. She'd been on nights two years!"

After another pause Plum told her about his resignation. Clearing his throat, he muttered, "Word got out in residential care circles about Cosham Glebe's what they called maladministration. Mostly the hand of Dorita alerting colleagues to nominate her nephew. With him in my shoes, up will go the rates at the Glebes in Chichester Brighton and Weymouth which, I regret to say, I had neglected of late in interests of getting Cosham up and running." Scratching his ear, he stared out at the turbulent sea, then sat up.

"Now, Beatrice, look at me? Do you think uncle has cottoned onto the fact of Will inside pouffe?"

"I can't say."

"The movers should be finishing up here pretty soon."

Outside Art's semi-bungalow, Plum got out of the car, crossed the paved area, peered through the pebbly glass and pressed the bell. Inside was shuffling until Dolly appeared, apologetic when she learned who he was.

"Jovian Plum from Mrs. Gorwick's former residence! How do you do? Here because her daughter, Beatrice, has expressed a wish to retain the pouffe left to her."

Art, inert on the studio couch, gave the nod.

Almost immediately Plum reappeared and handed the pouffe to Triss, who emptied contents on the seat. After a five-minute shuffle she sprinted up to the front door, leant on the Parfitt bell, tapped on the unlit window then rushed to the side gate, heaved herself up, jumped down the other side, entered the lean-to, picked up a pair of gardening shears, and threw open the back door bellowing, "Don't you tell me the Will isn't here!"

Art, unmindful of the sciatic nerve, leant far forward. The jolt to the lumbar region robbed him of breath.

Triss hovered overhead, "Since Mum's passing I have not felt Myself! With all the aggravation in my life, the one thing I could hold onto was my Peace of Mind!"

"Peace of mind!" Art jeered. "Your attention's always been on yourself and your cats and to hell with everybody else."

Heat coursed through recesses in Triss's neck and hairline. "All your attention's fixated on my mother's Will!" she screamed. "Sending over adult kids, with bouquets and teabags!"

Art choked, "What you're implying is disgusting." Holding his side, "Never in my life have I wanted one thing out of Ive. All along I've trained my kids in self-denial. The last thing in the world they need is charity." He took a deeper breath, "I was prompted by her need of a family sponsor. A blood relation."

"The principal blood relation is Me!"

"Your mum explained you can't handle money."

"She thought your way's small time."

"Small it might be but my way accumulates savings."

In the lull, an irregular ticking started up behind the living room wall and settled into a prolonged tattoo.

"Maw put herself out for Ive and Myrtle," Art informed the room. "Dressed 'em up in silk frocks with satin collars. Took 'em places. But not me! Oho no. Did Maw take Artie to the beach? To the parks? Not on your nelly! It was Ive who got my tea, cleaned me up, put me to bed. Someone had to." He wrinkled his eyes. "They took you out to buy new clothes. Had no one to smash up your dolls. Because you never had to fight is why you had three jobs and no spare cash! You could never handle family life so you take in cats!"

Triss lowered her head, eyes narrowing in the manner of Ivy, "As primary next of kin, I summon you to hand over that Will!"

"If I had it I might."

Triss charged round the room, dragged the tea table from the wall, upended armchairs, failed to shift the fish tank. Tore upstairs, threw open closets, scattered tins and bottles over the landing, spat at Art as with both hands she grabbed his shirt collar. He put one hand on her face, punched her in the mouth, lost his balance and fell, pulling her down, both tumbling on the stairs to where Art's right leg came to rest on Triss's abdomen. Breathing deeply, with superhuman strength and the use of her free leg, she wriggled free, knocking Art's head against a riser.

Outside on the low wall, she sat for some time before removing hat, scarf and coat, and rolling shoulders. Dolly, regaling Plum with the benefits of the Toyota engine, looked over now and then. Eventually, squeezing Plum's arm, she hurried back to the house. Plum, pulling down his watchcap, slammed the bonnet and, following in her footsteps, tapped on the unlocked front door.

Eventually Dolly showed up, holding what appeared to be a large ball of paper and pushed it on Plum. As he stood prolonging the Dolly handshake, Art, groaning, staggered between them, reaching for the papers.

"Oho no you don't!" Dolly shouted. "No, you don't understand. Allow me to speak. There's a hex on that Will! Oh yes. I'm up and down. Up and down! Since the day his sister died Art's been in pain. Has me up most hours every night. And running around most of the day! So please do Dolly a favour. Take this bloody Will out of my sight and leave the two of us in peace!"

As the front door closed, the living room clock started slowly to slide to the end of the mantelpiece, rocked a few times and tumbled with a clatter into the coal scuttle.

Plum made a final check of carburetor and spark plugs, then came over to Triss and bundled the Will into her satchel, mumbling, "The priority now is to get you something to eat." He helped her to her feet and saw her settled in the car. The car raced up the hill turning right at the main road and made for the first pub with bar food. Settled in the Troglodyte Saloon, Jovian ordered a half of Guinness, one lager shandy for Triss, and two platters of egg, beans and chips.

Triss sat without drinking and when the food's number came up, muttered, "In good conscience I cannot accept money I never earned. At fourteen, cold and frightened, she traipsed all over Milton with tenpence in her pocket."

In silence Plum finished his meal, washed it down with stout, then blotting his mouth, sighed, "Give a thought to the kitties, Beatrice! Vet care, boarding, diet foods. Should I read it out to you?"

"No, you don't understand."

He pulled over Triss's plate, finished it, took plates and his glass back to the counter, blotted the table with serviettes, carefully extricated the ball of stiff paper, running an arm across it several times.

As he did so, a coin dropped on the mat. Triss bent down and picked it up. It was a medal. Triss blinked at the inscription: "In honour of Sister I. Gorwick's rescue of toddler Ray from the hospital fire."

Plum read out, "'After expenses are defrayed comma to my daughter Beatrice and *all her cats* comma, is left the balance of my estate.' Beatrice, I'm driving you to your door."

"I've got a train ticket."

"I'm driving you."

"What about your partner?"

"Partner?"

"Your...wife? She'll wonder where you are."

"Ah! Mandy! My twin sister," he laughed, and shook his head. "Maybe I am what they say. A law-abiding joker. Helping Mandy in tiding over the death of her husband. She'll be returning to her flat."

"So, you're not married!"

"Was. To a fogey, too much like me. Lives in Chelsea. You see, Beatrice, up to now I've lived according to my dear mother's map."

A urinary twinge made Triss sit taut until she could safely get up and make it to the outlet. Eventually bolted in a cavernous stall, she tried emptying her mind as threads of stillness came in and, with them, a faint sense of peace, idly enfolding her; part-relaxing, part-energizing mother warmth. Something like support was coming in and with it interference, like old-time radio. Idly she blocked it out until a phrase caught her attention: *Fondue came out runny.* followed by: *Rendezvous to rake the nunnery.* Absorbed, she sat picturing a refectory with fondue served at a long table. After more crackling, a prolonged blank came in.

Eventually two maidens entered the facility, jolting the daughter and broadcasting news about agent outside. Ultimately Plum got clearance to enter and knock on the stall door until Triss came out and, leaning on him, was guided out. Settled in the Jaguar she gazed at the windscreen while Plum drove here and there, stopping the car to engage in spirited dialogue about the engine. When order was eventually declared, the car set off, flying past the Havant Rail Station turnoff.

For miles, Triss sat in range of Plum's droning. Then sliding into inattention, she felt a return of crackly intrusion and, somewhere near Guildford, words started up. She tried tuning in, gave up, then trying to relax, made out "*Take.*" And that, coupled with versions of "*Ceremony,*" eventually translated as "*it's yer money.*"

Night had fallen as the car reached West Hampstead along with

Jove's grievances about family and how they dubbed him *goyische Kopf.* Squeezing her shoulder, he turned off the engine, announced arrival at Dingley Gardens.

"Up to this day," he announced, "my life has followed the mold set by my dear mother. Today begins a new phase."

He handed her out of the car and across the main hall, and up two flights of stairs. At her front door, she fumbled in pockets, sorted through keys and unlocked. The minute her charges scampered out, she sank, making Jove hoist her in a fireman's lift, slouch in, settle her on a dining chair then, escorted by several cats, leave the room. After an interval, alerted by kitchen noises, the remainder trooped out, except the one treading her stomach. Dazed and remote Triss sat and sat until Jove returned with a mug of hot chocolate reporting almost all cat dishes found. "But no Rory!"

Triss, blurry eyed, sat vacant.

Dragging a chair close, Jovian murmured, "My dear, don't think I don't know what losing a mother is like!"

"I somehow…well…must have been…where I can't say…except another stratum…like now…. Where's my window?"

They sat close for a while until Plum said, "You're exhausted. And if you don't need me for anything, perhaps I ought to be on my way. An opening I heard about may be of interest to you. We can sound it out, maybe tomorrow?"

"What is tomorrow?"

"I believe it's Thursday."

"Why can't you tell me now?"

"Well, I've had enquiries from a few residences, one in North Wales, another in East Anglia. About looking into feline facilities in residential homes."

"What?"

"I don't know if you'd heard about feline comfort making its way onto the market! Certain elders, searching out residential care, are loth to leave kitty behind! Manses experimenting with systems. Doors with flaps. Trays collected. Clean up. Accommodating one kitty per room. So Beatrice, what do you say?"

"Well, I suppose it could have a ghost of a chance."

"I'm talking do-able. Like us in partnership?"

She started laughing and choking, eventually whispering. "My window's back."

"Well, well."

"All Mum had to say about cats was they don't bring in the do-re-mi!"

"Whatever your mother had to say might have been no more than an attempt to create a new meaning."

"In her opinion of me she created plenty of meanings."

"Anger is no more than love. The darkest deeds are committed without anger."

He drew Triss into a soft hug and as they stayed close, one of the tuxedos clambered up his jacket. It was Rory.

Settling down in bed with the Colonel, Triss was a schoolchild again: crouched in next door's newly-upgraded dugout, amid heavy ack-ack, bombs whistling, tiles falling, glass smashing, and Dad in a tin hat nodding at Mabel Harrison, the neighbour, with "I think that must be your house!" Mabel tipping up a narrow silver flask, throat pulsating.

Those nights under flares, tracer bullets, bombs and six pips announcing the nine o'clock news and Mum setting out to the hospital on her no-speed bike with tiny blue light, pedaling along dark, deserted roads, steering round earth clods and ignoring oaths and commands to get down in the ditch.

And oh, that afternoon in the evacuee schoolroom. Me at second desk from front! Never bothering to look up at doors opening or closing. But this time I had to look up! To what? Could it be right? To Her? Young and strong! Camel hair coat, chiffon scarf! Dark hair, dark eyes. Face powdered. My stuff in a carrier bag! Me burying my face in her coat, moaning: "Pinch me!" That day of days in November '39. On the train back to Portsmouth. Us.

Barbara P. Parsons

was born in Portsmouth, England, to a
naval family. After working overseas in
many different lands, she came to the
U.S. with her American husband in 1973.
She presently resides in Prince Edward
Island, Canada. She was active for many
years in green and animal liberation
issues, and contributed articles to *Sierra
Club's Wildlife Involvement News* and
edited the UFETA (Unitarians for Ethical
Treatment of Animals) newsletter.
Her novel, *Beulah Kettlehole and the
Patriarchal Ice,* was published in 2001.

Also by Barbara Parsons

Beula Kettlehole and the Patriarchal Ice

Barbara P. Parsons

Wickedly funny powers of observation, and the ability to translate those observations into vivid descriptions of people and places.
  — **Lucia St. Clair,** Author of *Ride the Wind*

In this droll and delightful novel Barbara Parsons gives us a rueful reminder that, from Bogotá to Broadway, women take dictation while men will always be men.
  — **Phyllis C. Robinson,** Author of *Willa, the Life of Willa Cather*

Set primarily against the backdrop of turbulent Colombia, BEULA KETTLEHOLE is an impressive and eloquent novel written with conviction and passion about one woman's struggle to rise above those who delight in degrading women.
  — **Murray Polner,** author of *No Victory Parades: The Return of the Vietnam Veteran*

…sad and funny novel in a colorful setting. Highly original.
  — **Wilma Shore,** author of O Henry Prize Stories

Beula Kettlehole

and the
Patriarchal Ice

Barbara Parsons